Calloway's Crossing

When Trip Kincaid saved Milton Calloway's life, Milton was so grateful he gave him his saloon at Calloway's Crossing. But when Trip arrived to claim his property, the saloon wasn't what he expected – it had in fact collapsed into a bubbling pool of mud!

Undeterred, Trip rebuilt the saloon. Within hours of opening, Ryan Trimble's protection gang muscled in on him and his only compensation was the distraction his bartender, the beguiling Grace Theroux, provided.

Trip needed help to defeat Ryan and it arrived in the form of a mysterious gunslinger – but at what price? Before long, Trip faced the fight of his life to not only save the saloon but also himself and Grace.

Calloway's Crossing

I. J. Parnham

A Black Horse Western

ROBERT HALE · LONDON

© I. J. Parnham 2006
First published in Great Britain 2006

ISBN-10: 0-7090-8083-2
ISBN-13: 978-0-7090-8083-1

Robert Hale Limited
Clerkenwell House
Clerkenwell Green
London EC1R 0HT

Typeset by
Derek Doyle & Associates, Shaw Heath
Printed and bound in Great Britain by
Antony Rowe Limited, Wiltshire

CHAPTER 1

Trip Kincaid crawled to the edge of the ridge and peered over a boulder at the campsite below. The situation was exactly as he'd feared.

Two bandits had bushwhacked a traveller. The poor man had probably invited them in to share his fire for the night, but instead they'd accosted him. Then, while one of the bandits held him at gunpoint, the other man ransacked through his possessions. Already clothes and utensils were strewn all over the site while the traveller stood with his hands thrust high.

By the light of the spluttering fire, Trip saw the tallest of the bandits tip the contents of a saddle-bag out at his feet, riffle through them with his foot, then hurl the bag away. He snorted with disappointment then gestured to his colleague, who strode a long pace to stand behind the traveller and jabbed his gun into the small of his back.

At the top of the ridge, Trip winced then drew his gun and stood. He wasn't a fast-draw gunslinger, but he considered himself deadly enough over short

5

distances. So to help this man he had to get closer. His main advantage was surprise and, as the night was moonless, the dazzling light of the campfire would mask his approach.

He paced down the slope, placing his feet to the ground slowly to avoid disturbing the grit and pebbles.

'Talk, now,' the tall bandit below him grunted, his harsh words coming to Trip on the light evening breeze.

The bushwhacked man struggled but found that the other bandit was holding him firmly and that the gun never wavered from his back. He desisted and glared at the bandit.

'About what?' he said, his voice defiant despite the desperate circumstances.

'You got to have something valuable.' The bandit spat on the ground. 'Give it to me.'

Trip had shuffled for over twenty paces down the side of the ridge, but he was still thirty yards from the bandits and had a complicated path around boulders and through gullies to negotiate in the dark. Although the dirt ahead looked loose and slippery, he speeded his journey downwards, pattering his feet with small steps to avoid falling. His lack of caution freed a flurry of pebbles that cascaded from under his feet, the low whisper of grit moving over grit being loud enough to herald his approach.

The tall bandit flinched then swirled round, his hand shooting up to his brow as he peered into the darkness. His colleague swung the captured man round to face up the slope and fired off a speculative shot.

The lead whistled by over twenty yards to Trip's side, but as he strode another pace and dislodged another flurry of dirt, the bandit homed in on his location and fired again. This time a slug cannoned into the dirt five yards ahead of Trip's feet.

Trip reckoned the next gunshot wouldn't be so wild. So he slid to a halt, steadied himself, and tore off a shot. The lead winged past the tall bandit's shoulder and in return both men crouched as they aimed up at Trip, who flinched away before either man could fire.

He saw the traveller use the distraction to tear himself away from the bandit who was holding him, but then Trip's feet slipped from under him, throwing him on his back. Two gunshots whistled over his tumbling form. Trip fought to right himself, but he couldn't find purchase in the loose dirt and he skidded down the slope on his back with his legs whirling in the air like an upturned beetle.

He dug his elbows in and grabbed at thin air as he tried to halt his tumbling, but still he slid downwards. A pained screech escaped his lips as his left elbow jarred against a rock.

Then Trip slammed into one of the many boulders on the slope. His head crunched into rock and a bolt of pain wrenched through him, as disorientating views of the night sky and the ground swirled around him.

Then the stars in the sky merged with stars that were closer to his eyes and the next he knew he was lying propped against a boulder at the bottom of the slope. A cold and wet cloth dampened his forehead, a flickering fire warmed his feet, and the man he had been trying to save was hunkered down before him and smiling.

Trip tried to get up, but had to fight down a gut-churning burst of nausea, and he slumped back down.

'Those bandits,' he murmured. 'We got to—'

The man placed a hand on his shoulder and bade him not to move.

'Relax,' he said. 'They're gone. You frightened them off.'

Trip fingered the cloth on his forehead. 'I slipped and banged my head. I couldn't have been that frightening.'

The man threw back his head and laughed then slapped his thigh, merriment twinkling his eyes.

'I know that now, but when you came hurtling down that slope a-hollering and a-screaming like the Devil himself was snapping at your heels, they thought the whole Seventh Cavalry was coming after them.' He winked. 'What you did wasn't that clever, but it sure was effective.'

Trip returned a snorted laugh then removed the cloth from his brow and sat up straighter.

'And what did they want?'

'What do any of them want? They just wanted what I had and would have got it if it hadn't have been for you. And I'm obliged for your help. . . .' The man raised his eyebrows.

'Trip Kincaid, and I'm glad I could . . .' Trip touched the back of his head, suppressing a wince as he located a tender bump, '. . . help.'

'I'm Milton Calloway.' He sighed. 'And I got no idea what I can give you to show my gratitude.'

'I never looked for nothing but that thanks,' Trip said, as Milton paced away to sit on the other side of the fire.

From Milton's grey hair and deep wrinkles, Trip judged him to be around fifty, and from his relaxed attitude, he judged him to be someone who had lived life to the full and who found enjoyment in any situation.

He watched him rub his chin then look up, nodding.

'But maybe there is something I can give you,' he mused. Milton leaned forward. 'Where were you heading before you threw yourself headfirst down that slope to save my life?'

'I came from over there.' Trip pointed over his shoulder then swung his hand forward to point down the trail. 'And I'm heading that-a-way.'

'Thought you looked like a travelling man, but have you ever thought of settling down?'

Trip considered then gave a slow nod.

'I guess I have. I've often thought it'd be mighty fine to have a stretch of land to call my own.' Trip blew out his cheeks as he considered some more. 'And I've spent enough time in saloons, so I guess I sometimes get a hankering to own one.'

Milton looked at Trip with his eyebrows raised then shook himself. He beamed a huge grin and slapped his thigh.

'A saloon, you say?' He raised his head to howl a cry of delight into the night. 'I just knew I was right to do this.'

While Trip considered Milton, wondering what he had in mind, his companion headed around the fire and sat beside him. He withdrew an envelope from his pocket. It was dirty and battered, but the parchment he slipped out had ornate writing and a thick seal at the bottom.

'You're giving me land?' Trip watched Milton as he continued to smile at him. 'A saloon?'

'Both.' Milton flicked the parchment open then turned it round so that Trip could read it by the firelight. 'A place where travellers like you can stop and enjoy a quiet drink along with fifty acres of the finest farming land you could ever want, if you're minded to use it. It's called Calloway's Crossing. A saloon so fine, it even carries my name.'

Trip took the offered parchment and after reading the first few lines saw that Calloway's offer was exactly as he'd suggested.

'I'm grateful, but if this saloon is that fine, why give it away?'

Milton's beaming smile died and he rolled onto his haunches to poke the fire. When he responded, no sign of his former good humour remained.

'I'll be honest with you. It's a burden. Two weeks ago I bet, won, and nearly got myself killed using it as a stake in a poker game. And I nearly ended up giving it to those two no-good varmints.'

'Don't let the likes of them tell you how to live your life.'

'I don't, but you're a travelling man with a hankering to settle down, and I'm a settled man who got himself a hankering to travel.' Milton looked down the darkened trail then sighed. 'Ever since I left Calloway's Crossing two years ago I've thought about the time I'd stop travelling and head back there, but now I reckon it's time to cut the ties and go my own way.'

While he pondered, Trip prodded the back of his head, probing around the sore spot. His first reaction of a refusal hovered on his lips as he searched for a way to decline the offer without hurting Milton's feelings.

But Milton's resolute gaze said a refusal would do more than hurt his feelings. He had faced death and had lost his self-respect. Giving Trip his saloon was the only way he'd restore that self-respect.

Moment by moment the temptation to accept Milton's offer grew until Trip ventured a smile.

'And where is this saloon?'

Milton slapped his thigh and grinned then pointed, the thrust of his arm indicating a general direction in the darkness.

'Stay by the railroad and keep going until you're about fifteen miles away from the friendliest town you could ever hope to visit – Wagon Creek.'

'It sure sounds fine.' Trip returned the grin and held out a hand. 'I *will* accept this saloon, and if you ever want to stop and rest while you're doing that travelling, you'll always have a friend at Calloway's Crossing.'

'And I'll do just that. I got a good feeling about you.' Milton took the hand and winked. 'I reckon this saloon and you were meant for each other.'

CHAPTER 2

Trip drew his horse to a halt before the rough sprawl of shacks, the wooden sign staked into the ground confirming he had arrived at Calloway's Crossing.

To his right was an expanse of pine. Behind him was a gentle hill, a creek heading down it to run past him to his left then around the shacks and lazily merge with a slow-moving river. The river's wide expanse captured the blue sky and returned a dazzling and cool reflection that would lift the spirits of the weariest of travellers. And the water was shallow enough and clear enough for Trip to see the stony bottom, suggesting this was the most convenient point for travellers to cross.

Trip couldn't see the saloon he now owned, but there was a trading post, a barn, a stable and an adjoining smithy splayed out on either side of the trail.

From within the smithy, Trip heard the crisp clang of metal on metal and he had the distinct but untroubling impression that somebody was watching him. And sure enough, after one final heavy clang, a brawny and soot-streaked young man emerged, wiping his hands on his apron.

The man sported a wide and hopeful grin, his teeth and eyes gleaming within his dirtied face, and hailed him, so Trip dismounted and stood beside the sign.

'Calloway's Crossing is a mighty fine-looking place,' he said, patting the sign.

The man introduced himself as Isaac Wheeler, then set his hands on his hips.

'It is at that. What can we do for you? We can provide most of what a man could want here without him even having to head through Wagon Creek.'

'A saloon would be fine.'

Isaac snorted. 'Except that. Pa can sell you supping whiskey to take with you, but if you want entertainment, you'll have to head to Wagon Creek.'

Isaac turned away, but Trip raised a hand, halting him.

'I wasn't looking for entertainment, just the saloon. Milton Calloway told me about it.'

'So you've met Milton Calloway,' Isaac mused. 'Suppose I'm pleased to hear that no-good dreamer is still alive.'

'No-good dreamer? When I met him he seemed a decent enough man.'

'Then he must have got religion because decent ain't a word anyone's ever used to describe Milton Calloway.'

Trip winced. 'You trying to tell me that Milton ain't a reliable source of information?'

'I am at that and plenty more besides.' Isaac

sighed. 'So what did Milton tell you about his *saloon*?'

Trip caught the emphasis on the last word, his guts rumbling with an impending sense of foreboding.

'He said he left it two years ago and . . .' Trip gulped as he saw a slow smile spread across Isaac's face. 'What's wrong with that?'

'Plenty. Milton left two *weeks* ago. He got into a poker game with his brother Adam and afterwards, Adam ran his no-good brother out of town with bullets a-flying everywhere. Milton wouldn't dare return.'

'He won't need to no more.' Trip took a deep breath then forced himself to smile and patted his bulging pocket. 'I own his saloon and land now. And it's all legal like.'

'You own . . .' Isaac considered Trip's fixed smile. 'You ain't joking, are you? You really do own Milton Calloway's saloon.'

A huge grin emerged as Trip nodded then Isaac hurried away into the trading post, his arms wheeling as he shouted out for his pa.

Chester Wheeler, a lean and stooped man emerged, his brow furrowed, but as he and Isaac walked towards Trip, Isaac spoke to him and slowly he matched Isaac's grin. He swung to a halt to stand before Trip and licked his lips, his eyes taking on a gleam.

'So,' he said, 'how much did you pay for Milton Calloway's saloon?'

'Nothing,' Trip said.

'Nothing!' Chester and Isaac exchanged an amused glance. 'Then Milton sure found himself a prize greenhorn, didn't he, Isaac?'

'He sure did,' Isaac uttered, his breath coming in short bursts as he fought to keep his amusement under control. 'Didn't think Milton would ever find an idiot stupid enough to pay that much for his property.'

Isaac and Chester threw back their heads and they both ripped out a loud snort of laughter then slapped each other on the back and laughed some more. They even linked arms and jigged around on the spot, kicking up the dirt and punching the air as they gave vent to their amusement.

'I don't know what you're laughing about,' Trip murmured when their first burst of merriment had died down, 'but Milton Calloway owned a saloon and a stretch of land around here.'

'He did.' Chester disentangled himself from his son's arm then rubbed his jaw and winced as if the laughter had made it ache. 'And how do you think Calloway's Crossing got its name?'

Trip pointed at the river, shrugging.

'Because it's the best place to cross the river?'

'Travellers *do* come here to cross the river. But I own most of the land around here, so why didn't I call it Wheeler's Crossing?'

'Don't know.'

Chester chuckled, prolonging the moment before he gave his answer.

'Because Milton Calloway double-crossed so many of those travellers that any fool who used the crossing ended up being crossed by Calloway.'

Trip rubbed his forehead as Chester and Isaac

whirled around on a new jig. He raised his voice.

'Be obliged if you stopped enjoying yourself now and just show me where my saloon is.'

Chester stomped to a halt then swung round to face the trading post.

'I sure will. I wouldn't miss this for anything.' Chester pointed at the post.

Trip narrowed his eyes, but couldn't see what Chester wanted him to see. So Chester beckoned him to follow him to the post and then around the side. Slowly the land behind the trading post opened up to his view. And between the meandering creek and the post there was an expanse of mud.

Trip closed his eyes a moment. 'Am I right in thinking that Calloway's land is the stretch of mud behind your trading post?'

'You guessed it.'

Trip walked to the edge of the mud and with his hand to his brow looked towards the river. As far as he could tell, the creek that ran into the river overflowed its banks frequently and it had converted the low-lying land to mud. Chester had had the sense to erect his buildings on elevated and dry land, but if Trip judged where he thought his land started correctly, he didn't have that luxury.

'Is all Calloway's land that muddy?'

'Nope. Nearer to the river, there's quicksand.' Chester laughed. 'Milton Calloway might have been the sneakiest, double-crossing varmint who ever lived around these parts, but he sure didn't have himself any sense or get much luck. He bought the only stretch of land around here that was of no use to man nor beast.'

'And the saloon?'

Chester beckoned Trip to follow him into the mud. They waded for three paces before the slurping mass pulling at their feet dragged them to a halt.

Chester gestured around him and Trip glared at the sodden and stinking earth, at first seeing nothing but the occasional bubble form then pop in the sea of mud. Then he noticed several rotting lengths of timber poking out.

'Calloway's Saloon,' Chester said, pointing at the strewn wood. He gestured with his arms outstretched, signifying a large structure, then flopped his hands over. 'It fell down, then sank.'

Trip sighed. 'I'm getting the idea that Milton Calloway ain't the most trustworthy man I've ever met.'

'He ain't. But he ain't the most useless man I've ever met because now this mud is yours, all yours.'

Trip hunkered down beside the longest whole length of wood he could find.

'Yeah,' he murmured, fingering the wood, then looked up to consider the expanse of mud before him. 'All this is mine.'

'Whiskey,' Trip grunted then slumped over the bar.

The bartender eyed Trip's hunched shoulders and downcast eyes with a rueful smile twitching the corners of his mouth. He pushed a full bottle and a glass to him then left him alone to his brooding.

But no matter how many times Trip poured himself a measure and knocked it back that brooding didn't lighten. He had travelled for two weeks along the side of the advancing railroad to reach Calloway's Crossing and all that effort had been wasted.

Trip prided himself on the fact that no man had ever got the better of him, but in this case Milton Calloway had. He hadn't hurt him or taken his money, but he'd taken something that was far more important: his time and his energy, and now the experience had sapped him of any idea as to what he could do next.

Even when he'd emptied half the bottle, he still couldn't accept his misfortune, but he did unburden his woes to the bartender, who returned supportive comments, although his lively eyes betrayed the fact he was remembering this tale and adding it to plenty of others featuring Milton Calloway's exploits.

But with his story completed, Trip felt ready to move on and he wended a path out of the saloon. On the boardwalk, he took a deep breath, noting that Calloway had been right about one thing – Wagon Creek was a fine town.

It was larger than Calloway's Crossing and the industrial sounds of hammering and sawing echoing around him suggested that before long this town would expand even more. The railroad was coming and Trip detected the barely suppressed excitement of the people that thronged the boardwalks about the forthcoming opportunities.

But he only wanted to leave Wagon Creek behind him.

He moved to his horse but, from the corner of his eye, he noticed that a woman had followed him out and was standing beside him. He stopped.

'You want me?' Trip asked, keeping his gaze on the road.

'I overheard your story,' the woman said, her voice amused and young, 'about you being the new owner of Calloway's Crossing.'

'I gave all the details to the bartender.' Trip turned to face the woman, noting the tight bodice, prominent bosom, and rouged cheeks of a saloon-girl. 'But I ain't in a good mood right now, so don't try to drag any fun out of me.'

A huge and beguiling smile emerged as she paced up to him, her eyes twinkling.

'Know this, Trip Kincaid – I've sent bigger men than you running out of town with their tails between their legs.' She chuckled, the gleam in her eyes suggesting this was true. 'But am I right in thinking you're leaving?'

'Sure am.'

She placed a hand on his chest then looped her fingers into his shirt and tugged him forward.

'Then before you go, I reckon I ought to show you something.'

Trip couldn't help but peer down the front of her bodice.

'And what's that?' he asked, licking his lips.

She released her grip to slap his arm, but only lightly, then headed off down the boardwalk, wiggling her hips.

'Follow me and you'll find out.'

Trip and the saloon-girl, who had introduced herself

as Grace Theroux, sat on a pile of rocks beside the creek. Below them was Calloway's Crossing with the creek heading down the hill until it flowed into the river, the water merging into the boggy patch of mud that was now Trip's land.

'I'm here,' Trip said. 'What you showing me before I go?'

Grace patted the rocks. 'These here rocks and this here creek.'

'And what about them?'

'You didn't drown your senses with your woes, did you, Trip Kincaid?' Grace pointed down the slope. 'Use your eyes and look.'

Trip wasn't in the mood for wasting time on idle speculation and he was on the verge of leaving. But then he noticed Grace's enticing smile and the entrancing way the sunlight reflected off the water and rippled across her clear complexion, and he realized how pleasant it was to spend time talking with such a friendly young woman. So he rolled to his feet and looked at the creek then at the rocks.

At first he couldn't see anything that interested him, aside from Grace. Then he looked over his shoulder and saw that behind him, the creek took a meandering course, but after the sprawl of rocks, it took a straight route down the hillside.

Trip looked down the hill then over his shoulder again. He winced. If the creek had continued on its general course, it would have flowed along a dry gully until it reached the river several hundreds yards away from his land.

But instead, it took an abrupt left turn.

'Somebody diverted the creek,' he said. 'And the creek took the quickest route to the river and that was over Calloway's . . . my land.'

'And without a gully to run down, it spread out and made a huge heap of mud.'

'Who redirected it?'

'Chester Wheeler. He needed to irrigate his fields and—'

'And I lost land and got a stretch of mud instead.' Trip slapped a fist into his other palm then put his hands to the nearest rock. 'But what Chester can put here, I can move.'

'You got a problem. Milton let him do it. When his saloon fell down the first time, he needed to raise money fast and Chester paid him to divert the creek.'

Trip raised his hands from the rock. 'And the second time the saloon fell down, was Chester involved?'

'Nope. Milton never figured the ground would get so muddy and one windy night it fell down, despite everything I did.'

'You did?'

'Yeah, I used to . . .' Grace fluffed her hair and raised her eyebrows. 'I used to tend bar for Milton.'

'And his saloon fell down just those two times?'

'Twice was bad enough, but that was Milton – a double-crosser, a dreamer, and a loser.' Grace looked down the winding expanse of the river. 'Fifteen years ago, Milton and Adam came here with money to start afresh. Milton frittered away his money – and plenty of other people's money – but his brother put time and thought into everything he did. He bought land ten miles downriver and now he's selling it to the rail-road for a fortune.'

'Obliged for the information.' Trip rubbed his chin as he considered Grace then smiled. 'You fancy trying to run a saloon again, but this time with a man who ain't a double-crosser, a dreamer, and a loser?'

Grace returned her enticing smile.

'I wondered when you'd ask.'

CHAPTER 3

'Didn't think you'd come back,' Chester said.

'I reckon I can make my saloon a success,' Trip said, dismounting.

Chester pointed towards Trip's land. 'And how will you do that? Build it on stilts?'

'Nope.' Trip signified that Chester should follow him then headed away from the trading post.

Chester watched Trip walk in the opposite direction to his land then snorted and followed him.

'You can't go over there. That's *my* land.'

Trip didn't reply immediately but carried on walking towards the dry gully that skirted around the edge of Chester's land.

'It is. But I want to show you something.' Trip paced down into the gully. He watched Chester edge from foot to foot then shrug and patter down the slope to join him. Trip knelt to finger the dirt. 'This gully is dry.'

'It is,' Chester said with his hands on his hips.

Trip hefted a handful of dirt then spat on it and slapped the muddy mess back to the ground.

'And my land is wet. But if the situation were reversed, my land would be dry and this gully would be wet.'

'It would,' Chester murmured, his tone cautious.

Trip stood and wrapped a friendly arm around Chester's shoulders then dragged him round in a circle. He gestured with an outstretched arm at the land beyond the gully.

'So I reckon you should give me a stretch of dry land.' Trip watched Chester closely. 'For a reasonable price, that is.'

Chester shrugged away from Trip's arm and kicked the dirt at his feet, sighing, then looked up.

'How reasonable?'

Trip rubbed his chin, feigning the consideration of a deep problem.

'Well, I got a saloon to build and stock out. And that's a problem because I've spent all my money in Wagon Creek.'

'Spent it on what?'

'I'd hoped you'd asked. I spent it on *dynamite.*' Trip pointed up the hill. 'And I gave it to my assistant and she's buried it in a heap of rocks up there and—'

Chester stomped two long paces and grabbed Trip's collar, but he didn't resist and let him drag him up close.

'What you threatening me with?'

'Release me before I count to five, or we'll be up to our necks in water.' Trip rolled his head to the side to look along the length of the gully and Chester followed his gaze until it alighted on the dam of rocks.

Grace chose that moment to bob up and wave.

Chester winced then swirled round to glare at Trip.

'That'll ruin my crops.'

'Only if you don't give me some land. One . . . Two . . . Three . . .'

'But I paid Milton to divert the creek.'

'You paid Milton, not me. Four . . .'

Chester snorted then threw Trip to the ground.

'I've released you, but I'll never give in to your threats.'

'Five.' Trip raised his hand a mite then lowered it and returned Chester's glare. 'What's it to be? Get wet or give me land for a saloon.'

Chester looked away, sighing. 'And then you won't blow up my dam?'

'You got it.'

'Then you got it.' Chester brushed by him and up the side of the gully. 'But somehow, I *will* make you pay for that.'

Trip rode into Calloway's Gulch, as the new railroad bridge was to be called, and what he saw impressed him.

The head of the railroad tracks was still fifty miles away, but at its unstoppable rate of progress, it'd arrive within a month. And the advance party of workers had already descended on Adam Calloway's land to build the bridge across the river.

Trip now saw the full extent of what Grace had told him about. Milton Calloway had settled in what at first glance had appeared to be an ideal location: a shallow crossing point of the river. But Adam had picked a seemingly inhospitable place to settle down.

The gulch was precipitous with the river swirling and eddying over the rocks below. But the water flowed rapidly because the gap between the two sides of the gulch was only thirty yards. And the solid rock sides were ideal for bearing the load of a bridge, and far better than the softer ground of Calloway's Crossing.

And when Trip crested the ridge to the north of the gulch to view the surrounding area, he saw the straight and gentle slope heading back east. And he judged that when they'd felled the trees, the land would need minimal work to convert it into an ideal route for a railroad.

Trip couldn't tell whether Adam Calloway had been a visionary in predicting where, one day, a railroad would go or whether he had been lucky, but either way, he had talents his brother didn't possess.

Trip headed into the site, where an army of workers was edging lengths of timber over the side to span the gulch. He located the foreman, Frank Moore, and learnt that Adam Calloway lived in a shack overlooking the bridge. He received an enthusiastic answer to his other question.

Then Trip headed up the wooded side of a bluff, the brown and white-flecked panoply of the river and great expanse of pines on either side of the river opening up to him. And when he reached the shack, Adam was standing on the edge of the sharp slope with the river surging by several hundred feet below. The huge drop didn't appear to concern him as he hailed him with an enthusiastic wave.

Trip joined him, although he kept ten paces away from the edge, and saw that Adam had the same build and twinkling eyes as his brother, and also the same assurance.

'Thought I ought to see you,' Trip said. 'I own your brother's land now.'

Adam snorted. 'How did that mistake happen?'

'I saved his life.'

Adam blew out his cheeks. 'If you want thanks, I'm not giving it.'

'Didn't look for that, but I thought you'd like to know he's fine and heading west the last time I saw him.'

'Don't care where he goes as long as he stays away from me. Have you heard about our poker game?' Adam watched Trip nod. 'Then you'll know he left town a few feet ahead of a hail of bullets, but I wish he'd been slower because that man will never learn.'

Trip hadn't known what kind of reception he'd receive, but felt he had to tell Adam about his brother. And he'd hoped to learn more details about Milton in case his saloon venture failed and he was minded to track him down. But now he felt only a desire to share his misery with a man who had been crossed by Milton all his life.

And so Trip unburdened his irritation, relaying the lies Milton had told him while looking down at the growing framework of the bridge below.

Adam was a good listener and despite his sullen lack of interest in discussing his brother, he sympathized in all the right places. When Trip had finished, he patted his shoulder.

'One piece of advice, Trip,' he said. 'Trust nothing my brother says or does, not ever, and especially when he asks for nothing in return.'

'What you suggesting?'

'I don't know, but that's the trouble with Milton. You never know what he really wants.' Adam turned away to contemplate the bridge that would earn him his fortune. 'He gave you his land for free, but with him, sometimes free is the highest price any man could pay.'

Trip rode back into Calloway's Crossing.

In the two days since he and Grace had formed their partnership, they had been busy, and while he'd been away, the fruits of their negotiations had been delivered. And Chester and his son were standing outside with their hats tipped back on their heads contemplating the timber lengths that would become Kincaid's Saloon.

Grace may have been a saloon-girl, but she was tough and was willing to work. She'd decked herself out in men's clothing and aside from a curvaceous figure, which the baggy clothes couldn't completely hide, the red bow tying back her hair was the only sign of her femininity. And she had already started work. Beside the dry gully on the opposite side of the trail to the expanse of mud, she had marked out a rectangle and was dragging the wood closer to it.

'Did Frank agree?' she shouted, straightening up.

'Sure did,' Trip said, as he dismounted. 'So we got five days to build us a saloon before our first customers arrive.'

'Five days! We can't build a saloon in—'

'And I thought you were the one who'd run a saloon before.'

Grace sighed, placing her hands on her hips.

'Yeah, yeah, I see you're learning fast. If the customers want it open in five days, we'll open in five days.' Grace pointed at the huge pile of timber to Trip's side. 'So don't stand around showing off your new-found knowledge, Trip Kincaid. I need help here or we *will* disappoint them.'

As Trip braced his back and shuffled his arms under the nearest plank, Chester and Isaac muttered to each other then joined them.

'What you mean about *customers*?' Chester asked. 'Milton served the passing travellers, like we do, but how can you know what customers you'll get in five days?'

Trip stood and tapped his forehead.

'Because I got more business sense than Milton ever had. A whole load of hard-working men are building the bridge over Calloway's Gulch. Come Saturday night, they'll get time off and they'll be mighty thirsty.'

Chester sneered. 'But they'll head to Wagon Creek for real entertainment, not come to this mud heap.'

Grace stepped forward and looked Chester up and down.

'You saying I don't know how to entertain hard-working menfolk?'

Chester gulped. 'I . . . I . . . I guess I'm saying that. . . .'

'From what I'm hearing, you're not saying noth-

29

ing. I can give them what they want here just as well as in Wagon Creek.' She watched Chester pale and Isaac go a vivid shade of red. 'As you both well know.'

Chester coughed and kneaded his brow, regaining his composure.

'What I am saying is that we don't need those sort heading here, shooting up the place, dallying with the likes of . . . of you, and raising all kinds of hell.'

'Hey,' Grace snapped, but Trip raised a hand.

'Don't take that attitude in front of a young lady. And remember, we can all gain from this. They could buy things from your post.' Trip ventured a placating smile, which Chester didn't return, so he lowered his voice. 'Then think about this – I've already invited them. Are you going to tell them they're not welcome?'

'No, but . . .'

'Then quit complaining. I'm sure we'll all get extra custom, and I'll keep things calm and orderly on Saturday, don't you worry.'

Trip ducked, letting the stool fly over his head and crash into the wall. He bobbed back up to confront the man who had thrown it, but then had to dance back to avoid another man who folded over the bar and tumbled to the floor on the other side. That man flexed his jaw then spat on his fist and vaulted over the bar to rejoin the fight.

Saturday night in Kincaid's Saloon was going much as Trip had expected it to.

The bridge workers had arrived an hour after sundown, announcing their arrival with much hollering and good-natured shooting. Chester had emerged to stand outside his door with a rifle held across his chest in defence of his property, but the workers had ignored him and piled into the newly built saloon.

Within the hour, they'd demolished a quarter of Trip's liquor and most of his furniture.

Then the real fighting had started.

But despite the mayhem, Trip judged that everyone was enjoying themselves. Already he'd earned enough to pay for most of his breakages and for the first time he saw how much money he could make from running a saloon – provided the fragile structure was still standing by the end of the evening.

Five days of hard work had gone into erecting the framework for the building, but only the front and back walls were complete. The side walls were just stretched cloth, which had now been shredded by men tumbling down into the gully when fights had overspilled.

'You coping?' he shouted to Grace, as he tried to serve three men at once.

'Yeah.' Grace paused from her serving for long enough to point to the door. 'But you got real trouble brewing.'

Trip glanced to the door and winced. Chester was standing in the doorway and surveying the chaos with his face bright red while snorting his breath through flared nostrils.

Trip signified that Grace should serve his next batch of customers, then wended a path through the heaving mass of brawling men to join him.

'Fancy enjoying your first drink in Kincaid's Saloon?' he said, holding a hand invitingly to the side.

'I do not,' Chester said, eyeing two fighting men who were standing toe to toe and slugging it out beside the door.

'But you must still be pleased. I bet Calloway's Crossing has never been this busy.'

'It hasn't, but I leave this sort of . . . of madness for the townsfolk of Wagon Creek to deal with. It should-n't happen in Calloway's Crossing.'

'This ain't madness. These are just hard-working men enjoying themselves.'

'I can see that, but what worries me more is the hard-working women in my barn.'

'Ah,' Trip murmured. He'd wondered what had happened to the saloon-girls Grace had collected from Wagon Creek earlier this evening. 'I hope you don't mind.'

'I *do* mind. I'm a family man with a son and a daughter and I don't appreciate having . . . having all sorts of goings-on going on in my barn.'

'I'll make sure that doesn't happen again.'

'You will do more than that. You will never bring the likes of these bridge workers here again.'

Trip looked over Chester's shoulder to peer up the hill in the dark.

'Before you take that attitude, remember that you destroyed my land.'

'I destroyed Milton's land with his misguided agreement, but if this is the alternative, I'll light that dynamite myself.' Chester set his hands on his hips.

'Tonight is Kincaid's Saloon's opening night, and it's its closing night.'

With studied finality, Chester turned on his heel and paced away. Trip watched him head back to his home then shrugged and hurried back to the bar where Grace was facing a dozen impatient and thirsty customers.

'What did he want?' Grace asked when they'd cleared the backlog.

'Well, he didn't want no drink that's for sure, but I guess he was saying we need to work harder at keeping everyone quiet.'

'We do, but . . .' Grace looked around.

Trip followed her gaze, noticing that a quiet and still zone was spreading around the saloon. And he immediately saw its cause.

Five newcomers stood before the door, casting measured glances at the customers. These men were packing guns and had the hard-nosed look of men who caused trouble even when they didn't have a drink inside them.

Trip was snapping a glance at Grace to prepare for serious trouble when the tallest man nodded to a customer, and this initiated a ripple of nodding and waves towards them.

Amidst the grunted comments, Trip heard the name Ryan Trimble uttered several times and he guessed that the tallest of the men, who stood at the front, was this man. He also guessed that he was a railroad supervisor and that everyone's deference meant he had authority over the workers even when they weren't working.

And as he looked at him, a half-forgotten memory battered at Trip's thoughts and told him he'd seen Ryan and maybe one of the other men before. But he shook that thought away and smiled as they paced across the room to stand before the bar, everyone that was in their way scurrying to clear away from their path.

'Welcome to Kincaid's Saloon's opening night,' Trip said.

Ryan considered the broken furniture, the smashed glass, the unconscious man sprawled over the end of the bar.

'And will it be your last night?'

'Nope. I reckon I've made enough to cover the damage. I'll be open for business to the railroad for as long as the workers want to come here.'

'I'm pleased to hear that.' Ryan smiled, but for a reason Trip couldn't identify, he felt his own fixed smile die away.

He gestured for Grace to serve Ryan, then stood back. But it was only when Ryan hunched over the bar that he recognized him.

He was the bandit who had bushwhacked Milton Calloway.

CHAPTER 4

Ryan Trimble's arrival in the saloon generated a permanent lull in the level of chaos. Although Trip didn't confirm his position at the railroad, the workers gave him and his men leeway, neither approaching them nor catching their eyes.

The poker games and chuck-a-luck proceeded as before, and the drinking continued at the same determined pace, but everyone limited their arguments to mild disagreements and didn't let their tempers flare.

For their part, Ryan and his companions maintained a boisterous circle of fun at the bar, chiding each other over matters that Trip didn't understand – not that he listened in on their conversation. But whenever anyone else raised their voice, Ryan's group looked in that direction and silence instantly returned.

Ryan didn't look at Trip with any more frequency than he would look at any bartender, so he didn't appear to have recognized him from their previous encounter. But then again, when they'd met it had been dark and Trip had been rolling down the side of a ridge and screeching in pain.

After midnight, small groups headed away, thinning out the saloon. Later, a wagon rolled up. Many of the customers who were too drunk to make their own way back to the bridge staggered into it to roll out of town accompanied by much liquor-fuelled bawdy singing and good-natured shooting.

This left around a dozen men and, with the main bulk of workers having left, the saloon-girls wandered back into the saloon from the barn, flustered and weary, but smiling.

'Mighty pleased you invited us,' the buxom Sally said, then patted a bulge beneath her bodice that Trip presumed contained a considerable stash of money.

'I said it'd be more profitable out here than back at Wagon Creek,' Grace said, then took her hand.

Trip saw a flash of green as bills changed hands. He'd gathered that Grace would take a cut of the women's earnings, but he'd decided that as she'd already done him more favours than he could repay, he'd let her profit from this on her own.

She moved on to surreptitiously take money from the other two women, Melanie and Wanda, while offering support for their hard work.

'And you'll come back next week?' she said, after making their cuts disappear into her clothing.

'If it's this good, sure.' Sally flashed a glance at Trip then turned to leave, but a bleary-eyed drunkard, Lee Johnson, was standing in her way.

'You forgot about me,' he said, slurring his words.

He wheeled his arms and planted his feet wide to avoid falling over.

'I didn't,' Sally said. 'You've already had your turn.'

'That was with that one,' he said waving a finger in Melanie's general direction. 'It wasn't with you.'

Sally sashayed up to him and planted a firm finger on his chest then pushed, knocking him back a half-pace.

'Then remember, I'll be here next week and waiting for you if you got the money to pay.'

'I got the money to pay *now* and I don't want no waiting.'

Sally sighed as Grace and the other women joined her and, with the solid phalanx of rouged and buxom women facing Lee, they tried to stare him down, but he was beyond behaving reasonably and he lunged for Sally.

Before Trip could react, Grace thrust out an arm, grabbed Lee's elbow, and yanked it up his back, spinning him round in the process.

She pulled him back to her chest then hissed something into his ear that caused Lee's eyes to boggle and his throat to shake with a pronounced gulp. Then she threw him away towards the door.

He staggered to a halt, kicked at the floor, then, with his shoulders slumped, wended a path to the door.

By the bar, Ryan laughed at his predicament.

'Perhaps I ought to hire her to build the bridge,' he shouted after him. 'She's more ornery than you are.'

Ryan's men laughed with more enthusiasm than his weak joke warranted as Lee stopped, straightened, then turned. With deliberate paces, he strode back to the women, his breath coming in harsh snorts and his face bright red, but Grace stood before him ready to repel him.

Trip reckoned Grace could take care of this drunkard and he judged that an important test of her ability to keep control was getting underway. So he stayed by the bar and watched her pace to the side, keeping Lee in view.

Lee lurched round to follow her, his arms wide and his movements unsteady. Then he lunged for her, but the move was slow and wild, and she easily ducked under his flailing arm and when she came up, she delivered a kick to the rump that piled Lee into the bar.

More laughter ripped out, adding to Lee's discomfort and, when he rolled to his feet, his mouth was set in a grimace and his red-rimmed eyes were wide and staring. Still, Grace stood before him and even beckoned him on.

But Ryan and one of his men, Pike, brushed past Trip and the watching women to stand behind Lee. Ryan slapped a hand on his shoulder and spun him round.

'She says,' he grunted, 'she doesn't want you.'

'I can take care of him,' Grace said, but Ryan didn't even look at her as he fixed Lee with his firm gaze.

'You,' Lee muttered, standing up to Ryan, 'can't tell me what to do when I ain't working.'

A sharp intake of breath rippled round the onlookers, and Lee himself winced as he appeared to suddenly realize who he'd just threatened.

'I can, assuming you want to work again.' Ryan flashed a harsh smile. 'Or to breathe again.'

Lee gulped. He glanced at Grace then at the nearest onlooker, who shook his head. He took deep breaths then waved in a dismissive manner at Ryan and slouched off on a snaking path to the door.

Ryan turned on the spot, holding his hands high and signifying that he'd resolved the argument and now everyone should leave. He tipped his hat to Grace, who returned a curt nod, then slapped a hand on the bar and ordered another drink.

As Trip served him, most of the remaining customers filed out of the saloon. Two of Ryan's men also left, but the rest stayed.

Trip saw that Grace was talking to the other women and detected from her hunched shoulders and shortness of tone that she wasn't happy with having her authority usurped. And Trip detected some uneasiness in himself, but judged that being nice to people he didn't trust would be a part of his new life as a saloon owner and he maintained his smile.

Presently, he heard raised voices outside. He glanced at Ryan, but he'd returned to talking with his remaining colleagues. Grace and the women were already heading to the door to investigate.

Trip followed them and outside, he saw that a fight was underway in the area between the saloon and the back of the barn.

The stragglers from the saloon had stayed to watch and had formed a loose circle that at first didn't let Trip see who was involved. But when he moved closer he saw that one of Ryan's men, Heath, was holding Lee upright while Pike administered a firm pummelling, knocking Lee one way then the other. And the barely conscious Lee couldn't muster the strength to defend himself.

'That's enough,' Trip shouted, advancing on them.

Pike broke off from hitting Lee to glance at the approaching Trip.

'It ain't.' Pike looked in a steady arc around the onlookers. 'Everyone needs to see what happens if they talk back to Ryan.'

Pike paced in and delivered a short-armed jab to Lee's guts that had him folding and spitting bile over his boots.

Trip hurried to the circle, and as Pike flailed two round-armed punches into Lee's face, fought his way through to stand before Pike.

Heath signified that Trip was raising his fists and in response Pike raised his hands high and put on a mocking smile.

'Hey,' he said, backing away a pace, 'we're just keeping the peace.'

'This ain't any kind of peace I know,' Trip grunted, stomping towards Pike and rolling his shoulders. 'Leave him.'

Pike considered Trip's belligerent stance then glanced at Heath, who snapped his arms upright to leave Lee standing and swaying. Pike turned away, but then snapped round and with a solid pile-driving blow hammered Lee's cheek, sending him reeling into the dirt.

Pike batted his hands together and turned to face Trip.

'I've left him. Any problems?'

Trip snorted his breath through his nostrils, but a man from the circle paced forward and rested a hand on his shoulder.

'Walk away,' he whispered, 'while you and Lee still can.'

Trip looked around, noting that Ryan was leaning on the saloon doorframe, eyeing the situation. He sighed and acknowledged the sense, if not his desire to do this, then headed past Pike to kneel beside the unconscious Lee.

With the confrontation ending, the rest of the onlookers broke up, although Chester and his son emerged from the trading post to join him.

Chester didn't look at Trip as Isaac confirmed that the beating had been serious enough for them to take Lee to the barn to check out his injuries. Trip offered to help, but Chester just sneered at him.

'We've had enough of your *help* tonight,' he snapped. He took Lee's shoulders and Isaac took his legs. As they manoeuvred him to the barn, Trip headed over to Ryan.

'Your men didn't have to beat him that badly,' he said.

'He'll get over it soon enough if he wants to earn enough to eat,' Ryan said. He provided a huge smile that didn't reach his eyes, 'And don't you worry.

You're under my protection now and nobody harms you or your business, or they answer to me.'

And with that promise, Ryan gathered his men around him and they followed the rest of the customers in heading out of Calloway's Crossing.

Grace joined Trip to watch them leave.

'You didn't thank him,' she said.

Trip sighed. 'That's because he wasn't doing me no favours and I reckon I'll be paying plenty for that protection.'

Trip spent a sleepless night wondering whether Ryan's promise of protection was the bad news he feared it might be. In the morning, he was no clearer as to whether it was and what he should do about it.

He mooched around the saloon, feeling unenthusiastic about clearing up last night's mess, and finally sat on the planks he had yet to use on the edge of the gully. Chester had given him land on the top of the bank, so Trip could sit with his back resting against the saloon's back wall and with his legs stretching down the bank into what, if the creek still ran this way, would be water.

Today he'd planned to work on a third wall, but was lethargic about doing that, too, and he leaned on his knees as he peered into the gully, his mind drifting as he avoided dwelling on his problems.

Halfway down the bank was a pile of freshly turned earth. Trip couldn't remember throwing the soil they'd dug out for the foundations this way and he shuffled down the bank to consider the dirt. He decided that a burrowing animal had dug into the bank and had thrown the earth behind it as it made a home for itself beneath the saloon.

He knelt and searched for the hole it'd made, but then stood, accepting that he was only interested in discovering what the animal was to avoid facing up to the bigger problem he had to deal with today.

And with that thought, he headed to the barn to check on Lee. Isaac was tending to the injured man and he looked up at him, snorted, then shooed him away.

'He'll be fine,' he said. 'He's getting the best care a man could want – no thanks to you.'

Trip winced as he looked at Lee, who lay on his back, his features puffy and unrecognizable, and the mottled mixture of cuts, scrapes and emerging bruises told the story of every blow Pike had inflicted on him. Then he considered the care with which Isaac was cleaning a long scrape.

'You're a talented man.'

'Got to be to earn a living at a place like Calloway's Crossing.'

'Not get many people pass by, then?'

'Railroad is bringing more, but most people still prefer Wagon Creek.'

'Then we got to attract more.'

Isaac provided a knowing smile. 'You know Pa's view on that.'

'I do, but it doesn't have to be yours.'

Isaac opened his mouth, and although Trip reckoned the young man was about to offer support, he closed it and returned to dabbing at Lee's bruised ribs. Beneath his gentle touch, Lee emitted a groan although he didn't open his eyes.

Trip considered sharing his fear about Ryan with the potentially sympathetic Isaac, but decided he didn't want to risk the news reaching Chester. He patted Isaac's shoulder, offered him encouragement, and headed to the door. But he stopped in the doorway to glance at Lee and offer a silent prayer for him to get better.

Either that prayer was answered or Lee was more resilient than he'd feared because later that morning, when Trip had cleaned out his saloon and was preparing to head to Calloway's Gulch, Lee emerged from the barn to accompany him.

No customers had visited on this fine Sunday morning and with Grace having returned from Wagon Creek, Trip left her in charge.

As he mounted his horse, one man did meander into town from across the river. He was hunched and silent, repeatedly yawning. Trip tipped his hat to him, but he didn't acknowledge him as he headed past him, dismounted, then slouched into the saloon.

Trip decided that Grace could readily deal with this placid customer and, with Lee, headed off. On the way, he pressed the morose man for details about Ryan and his role at the railroad, but Lee wasn't prepared to talk about him. And when they reached the bridge, he hobbled off to join the other workers without even a backward glance or one word of thanks for his help last night.

Trip saw no sign of Ryan, so he located Frank Moore, the bridge foreman, to see if he had more interest in the subject of Ryan's behaviour than Lee had.

'You had trouble last night, I heard,' Frank said, after they'd exchanged pleasantries.

'Nothing I couldn't handle.' Trip took a deep breath. 'But then Ryan Trimble provided his *help*. And I ask myself why.'

Frank considered Trip then swung round to gesture to the bridge then east along the route the railroad would take.

'Taking care of this is a mighty big job. We work seven days a week, non-stop. And I need men with all sorts of skills.'

'And Ryan's skills?'

'Since he's joined us, he's kept people quiet and when people are quiet, the railroad gets built. That explain?'

'All too clearly. And what do people like me who don't want to be quiet do?'

Frank snorted a laugh. 'They remember this – the railroad payroll is overdue and my men spent the last of their money with you last night. Now they're getting itchy. But twenty thousand dollars arrives tomorrow to pay them and to pay off Adam Calloway. I need muscle like Ryan around in case anyone reckons they'd like that money for themselves. So if you got a problem with Ryan, I ain't listening.'

Trip sighed. 'I guess I can see that.'

Frank fixed Trip with a firm glare then softened his expression and swung round to look eastwards.

'But in a month, the bridge will be built, the railroad will have moved on, and me, Ryan and the rest

45

will have moved on with it. If you got a problem with him, just prevail awhile.'

Trip thanked him for the advice then left, but, when he rode out of the gulch, he swung away from the river to head to Wagon Creek.

Frank's advice was guarded but sound, and it had also confirmed his worst fears.

Ryan dealt in violence and the railroad needed people like him to run their operation smoothly. And even when Ryan extorted money from the people along the railroad's route, Frank wouldn't intervene.

So he had to involve the law.

Early in the afternoon, he rode into Wagon Creek and headed to the town marshal's office.

Marshal Kaplan was in and enjoying a siesta. His bulging paunch, sparse grey hair, and food-splattered clothing didn't fill Trip with optimism. And when his knocking on the desk finally roused the marshal and he raised his hat, his sagging jowls and bored acknowledgement of his presence dampened his spirits even more.

'I reckon I got me a problem,' Trip said.

'You only reckon, eh?' Kaplan drawled, then delivered a wide yawn with his arms thrown wide. He rocked his feet down to the floor and shuffled his chair closer to the desk until his substantial belly pressed against it. 'Tell me all about it if you must.'

Trip ignored Kaplan's less than enthusiastic tone and leaned his hands down on his desk to share his eye-line.

'Ryan Trimble keeps the bridge workers at

Calloway's Gulch in line with intimidation,' he said, settling for plain speaking to a man who ought to be more inclined to resolve his problem than Frank had been. 'And I reckon he's not averse to meting out punishment to anyone along the railroad's path.'

Kaplan nodded, his jowls shaking. 'And?'

'And I thought you'd like to do something about it.'

Kaplan's small eyes blazed. 'Now why would I want to do that?' Kaplan signified that Trip should stand back then folded his flabby arms on his desk. 'I'll tell you how it works. The railroad is a-coming and that's good for Wagon Creek. We're booming and there's talk of electing a mayor and a sheriff and of expanding to satisfy all the new people who'll flock here.'

'That's for the future. What about the people who are suffering from the railroad now?'

'That's the price of progress.' Kaplan flashed a smile. 'Understand?'

Trip searched for something to say to clarify his fears, but then saw that anything he said would just waste his breath. Marshal Kaplan was old and was used to keeping the peace in a town that never saw trouble. He wasn't equipped for dealing with the likes of Ryan Trimble and, as he was serving out his time until the appointment of a sheriff, he saw no reason to trouble himself. So he'd sit in his office, collect his stipend, and dream away his time until he could retire.

'Yeah, I understand you.' Trip tipped his hat, turned his back on the yawning marshal, and headed to the door.

With nobody else to turn to, Trip returned to Calloway's Crossing.

On the way, he tried to console himself with the thought that maybe he'd overstated the problem with Ryan, but when he arrived back at the saloon, those hopes died.

A line of horses was outside the saloon, and they included Ryan's bay.

CHAPTER 5

Trip headed into the saloon to see that Ryan and his men were sitting around the only whole table that the mayhem of the previous night hadn't destroyed. They were passing a jug of beer around and, in their haste to drink, spilling most of it on the floor.

The only other customer was the man who'd headed into the saloon before he'd left and who was sleeping on the floor with a blanket drawn up to his chin. With a wry smile, Trip noted that even Ryan's ribald shouting wasn't rousing this man from his slumbers, then kept the smile on his face and the faint inkling of good humour on his mind as he paced inside.

'Everything fine?' he asked Grace at the bar.

Grace pointed to the sleeping man. 'He's been no trouble. Can't say the same about the others.'

'And what about. . . ?' Trip noted that Grace was nodding, signifying that Ryan had left the table and was approaching. Trip maintained his smile as he turned to face him. 'You enjoying yourself?'

'Sure am,' Ryan said, the half-empty jug of beer

dangling from his hand. 'You came to the bridge, asking about me. So I came here, asking about you. Perhaps now we can talk to each other.'

'Perhaps we can. I like plain speaking.'

'Then I'll give you some. I protect the railroad.' Ryan jabbed a finger against Trip's chest. 'And now I protect you.'

Trip nodded. 'And how much will this *protection* cost me?'

Ryan rubbed his chin as if he was considering, although the gleam in his eye suggested he'd already decided.

'Fifty dollars a day. And I'll keep trouble away from you and nobody will threaten your business.'

Trip firmed his jaw as he faced up to Ryan, but Grace darted forward to stand between them.

'We're obliged,' she said.

'You sure?' Ryan said, his gaze directed over Grace's shoulder and never leaving Trip. 'Because I don't reckon Trip likes my offer.'

'He likes your offer.' She turned and raised her eyebrows, her concerned gaze imploring him to avoid trouble. 'Don't you, Trip?'

'I do *not* want protection,' Trip grunted, 'but I do want to tend my bar and serve my customers, and right now they include you. So do you and your men have everything they want?'

Ryan glanced back at his men and mouthed something that dragged a laugh out of them. Pike peeled away from the table and headed outside. The rest swung round to face him with eager grins plastered over their swarthy faces. Trip watched Pike leave until

Ryan drew his attention back to him with an arrogant click of his fingers.

'We have,' Ryan said, licking his lips. 'But you still ain't agreed to my terms.'

'And I never will.'

Ryan rolled his eyes, and Trip bunched his fists ready for the fight that had to be close, but instead, Ryan hurled the jug over his shoulder. It crashed to the floor, splashing a fountain of beer in all directions. Ryan glanced back at it then shrugged.

'If that's the way you want to deal with me, then I'm your customer and I need more beer.'

Trip glanced at Grace, but she returned a slow shake of the head, so he gritted his teeth and placed another jug on the bar.

'Enjoy,' he grunted.

Ryan considered the jug then roared with anger and swung both arms to the side. He swept the jug to the floor, dragging several other glasses with it, then batted his hands together and turned back to Trip.

'I said – get me more beer.'

Trip rolled his shoulders, ready to start a fight he probably couldn't win, but Grace faced up to Ryan while holding an arm back, ensuring Trip kept his distance.

'Now, now,' she simpered, providing her most disarming smile. 'Do you really want to waste all our beer? Wouldn't you prefer to enjoy yourself?'

'I am enjoying myself. In fact I want all your customers to enjoy themselves.' Ryan roved his arrogant gaze around the saloon until it rested on Trip's only other customer, the sleeping man. A wicked gleam lighted his eyes as he swung round to face him. 'Hey, you, are you enjoying yourself in Kincaid's Saloon?'

As Ryan's men sniggered, Trip took a pace backwards and firmed his jaw, accepting that Grace was right and that he didn't want to provoke a confrontation now when he was so outnumbered.

He watched as, with a sly grin emerging, Ryan headed across the saloon to stand over the sleeping man. He tapped a foot on the floor, but the man returned a snore from beneath his hat.

'I said,' Ryan demanded, 'are you enjoying yourself?'

A low, rumbling snore escaped the man's lips.

'Now,' Ryan roared, his eyes blazing, 'who are you to sleep when I'm asking you a question?'

The man lay back, his hat over his eyes and deep snores rasping from his throat.

'I said,' Ryan persisted, toeing the man's ribs, 'who are you to ignore me?'

Ryan snorted his breath, receiving another prolonged snore, then glanced back at his men with his face reddening. The men returned incredulous stares and urged him to kick the sleeping man awake, so he swirled round and kicked the man's blanket away.

As the blanket flew away, Trip saw that under the blanket, the man had crossed his arms over his chest, but in his right hand he held a cocked gun. And with a snap of the wrist, the man swung it up to aim at Ryan. Then he raised his left hand, extended a finger, and pushed up his hat to reveal eyes that were open and which fixed Ryan with a cold gaze that said he wouldn't lose a moment's sleep if he were to pull the trigger and blast him away.

'Who wants to know?' he drawled.

Ryan returned his gaze. 'The name's Ryan Trimble.'

'Obliged.' The man drew his hat back over his face, reached down for his blanket, and laid it over his chest. Presently, a huge snore ripped out.

Ryan stood back, still looking down at him, then laughed. He swaggered back to the bar, repeatedly chuckling.

Trip braced himself, expecting that to save face Ryan would be even more determined to provoke a fight with him, but when he returned, he calmly picked up the remaining jug from behind the bar and returned to his men. He placed it on the table. Heath lunged for it and started to drink, but Ryan yanked it from his hand while he was pouring the beer down his gullet. As the beer sprayed everywhere, Heath grunted with annoyance then lunged for the jug.

Then the two men jostled each other, and the others taunted them as the group returned to providing their own boisterous entertainment, the confrontation with Trip forgotten for now.

Trip joined Grace in leaning back against the wall behind the bar. They watched the unruly men cajole each other in between flashing concerned glances at each other as they waited to see what form the next confrontation would take.

The latest jug of beer was still being fought over

when, through the window, Trip saw Isaac Wheeler hurrying towards the saloon. Nearer to the barn, his father was scurrying around, darting his gaze through the barn door and hurling his hands high in exasperation or perhaps shock.

Trip headed to the door to investigate and when he threw open the door, Isaac's wide and staring eyes confronted him.

'Fire!' Isaac shouted, the tang of burning accompanying his cry.

Trip looked over Isaac's shoulder to see tendrils of smoke rising from the barn. He turned to request Grace's help, but she was already running past him. Loitering by the barn was the sniggering Pike, but Trip ignored him and hurried after Grace.

If the creek had still followed its original route, they could have ferried water easily, but instead they needed to go to the river and back. Chester and Grace grabbed buckets and ran off on the journey while Trip and Isaac headed into the barn.

Luckily, the fire was only consuming a pile of hay by the wall. Despite the lack of water, they were able to use pitchforks to drag the burning pile into the centre of the barn where it could burn itself out. Then they used brooms to beat out the stray flaming stalks and although the fire was consuming the lowest planks in the wall, Chester and Grace returned with water. Several well-directed buckets extinguished the flames, leaving the only losses, aside from their frazzled nerves, being the hay and a wide scorch mark on the barn wall.

When they were satisfied they'd averted a potential disaster, they left the barn, breathing heavily, to find Pike was still outside, appraising their endeavours.

Chester cast suspicious glances at him then with his son headed to the post, leaving Trip and Grace to return to the saloon.

'You dealt with that trouble real well,' Pike said, grinning.

'Yeah,' Trip said, stopping ten yards from the saloon to glare at him. 'No thanks to you.'

Pike shrugged. 'I would have helped, but as I ain't been paid, I didn't.'

'I only hire the best, not two-bit varmints like you.'

'You'd better hire me. Because the next time Ryan gives the word, if I ain't been paid, I might burn the whole barn down. And if you're really unlucky, someone might even get trapped inside.'

'And if you're really unlucky, that person could be you.'

Pike set his hands on his hips as he faced Trip.

'I can't wait for Ryan to give that word,' he said, sneering, 'because I'll enjoy doing to you what I did to Lee last night, except I ain't ever going to stop.'

Pike spat on the ground then headed to the saloon, and Trip was about to follow him when Grace leaned towards him.

'Laugh,' she whispered, then moved back.

Trip glanced at her, furrowing his brow, but then laughed and Pike swirled round to see Grace jerking away from Trip and grinning at him.

'What did she say to you?' he demanded.

Trip had no choice but to shrug, but Grace took a

pace forward.

'Just something one of the girls said about you last night.' She chuckled. 'And having seen you again, I reckon it has to be true.'

Pike's face reddened, his fists opening and closing, and when Trip laughed again, he roared with anger and charged at Trip with his head down, aiming to bundle him to the ground.

Trip stood his ground then, at the last moment, jumped aside, but Pike lurched out an arm and grabbed a loose grip of Trip's waist that pulled Trip round and his momentum dragged them both to their knees.

They swung round to face each other. Pike threw the first punch, landing a blow on Trip's cheek and Trip returned a straight-armed jab to Pike's chin. On their knees, neither blow landed with much force, so Trip rolled back on his haunches and stood.

Pike followed him and jumped to his feet, but walked into a swinging uppercut to the chin that cracked his head back. But Trip didn't let him fall. He grabbed his shoulders and stood him straight then slammed a scything blow to his cheek that wheeled him to the ground.

'That was for Lee,' Trip said as Pike lay on his back, shaking his head and fingering his jaw.

His taunt made Pike's eyes blaze with anger and he rolled to his feet, but this time slower than before. He stormed in, flailing his fists and hoping to subdue Trip with his berserk action, but Trip kept his gaze firmly on Pike's fists and danced lightly on his feet as the blows came.

He ducked below long hay-making punches and swayed back from the jabs. Each missed blow only made Pike's anger grow, but his strength weakened. So when Trip had weaved away from yet another blow, this one making Pike stagger round until his back was to him, Trip paced in with both hands clutched together and hammered his fists into the back of Pike's neck. The blow knocked Pike to the ground, burrowing his face into the dirt.

Pike lay a moment, snorting his breath, then staggered to his feet bent double, but Trip was waiting for him and he crunched a low blow into his guts that had him spluttering and staggering round on the spot.

'And that was for the fire,' Trip said, as Pike stomped around, whining.

Trip waited with his fists raised for Pike to face him again, but Grace moved in and with a speed and a deadly accuracy that surprised Trip, she kicked out. Her boot landed a blow between Pike's legs that turned his legs to jelly and had him dropping to the ground to grind his forehead into the dirt and bleat out his pain.

'And that was for not letting me deal with Lee my way,' she said, then turned to Trip and put on a sweet smile that was in direct contradiction to the devastating blow she'd just struck.

'So,' Trip said, 'am I right in thinking that this is the right time to start that fight with Ryan, then?'

She nodded. 'One down, four to go.'

Trip returned her nod then turned to the saloon, but it was to face Ryan and a drawn gun.

57

'Seems you know how to use your fists,' he said, glancing at the sprawling Pike from the saloon doorway. 'You got the same skill with a gun?'

Trip set his feet wide. 'My gun's behind the bar. I'll fetch it if you want.'

Ryan beckoned for Heath and another man to drag Pike back into the saloon then considered Trip.

'All I want is fifty dollars a day and you'll get no trouble. So either come in and avoid that trouble by paying me, or come in and collect your gun and get more trouble than you can deal with.' Ryan glared at Trip then backed away into the saloon, leaving Trip and Grace alone.

Trip stared hard at the saloon door, pondering various courses of action, then pointed out of town.

'Grace,' he said, 'this is where you head back to Wagon Creek.'

She snorted. 'I'm going in there with you.'

He shook his head and moved to walk past her, but she grabbed his arm and clung on. Trip continued to glare at the saloon, then slowly turned to her.

'I've seen that you can take care of yourself, but I got some serious business to deal with in there and this could get—'

'Don't give me any of that tough talking nonsense, Trip Kincaid,' she said, her voice low and imploring, her eyes watering. 'I've spent enough time with you to know the kind of man you are, and Ryan's more trouble than you can handle alone. Accept you need my help, and perhaps even Chester and Isaac's help.'

'I *do* need help running the saloon, but you accept one thing.' He laid his hand on hers, squeezed it, then lifted it from him and walked away. 'On this, I won't accept it from you.'

'Trip Kincaid, wait!'

He stopped. 'Why?'

'Because ... because I don't want you to get killed.'

Trip swirled round and held his hands wide.

'Then what do you suggest I do?'

Grace closed her eyes as, from the saloon, raised voices and the crash of a smashed jug sounded, the commotion only helping to convince Trip he had to deal with Ryan now. But the noise heralded the arrival of the man who had been sleeping. This man wandered out of the saloon and slouched towards his horse without looking at them, still yawning repeatedly.

'We need a proper plan,' she said, then pointed at the man. 'And I reckon we start by getting the right sort of help.'

'You can't mean him, can you?' Trip said, as the man walked his horse away from the saloon with his head down.

'Yeah. You saw the way he drew his gun and faced down Ryan.'

'I saw the way he'd already drawn his gun then went to sleep.'

'Trip Kincaid, just leave the thinking to me,' she said, then hurried over to stand before the man. 'You enjoy your stay,' she asked, 'Mr. . . ?'

The man stopped, looked up, and provided a slow nod.

'Baxter Riley, and it's a fine place,' he drawled.

'Let's hope Ryan doesn't shoot you up. Can't do no sleeping with all that shooting going on.'

'You can't.' Grace laughed, the sound light and unconcerned. 'But I reckon you could sleep through anything.'

'Yup.' Baxter delivered a last enormous yawn then turned to mount his horse, but Grace edged to the side to stand before him.

'I was wondering . . .' She took a deep breath. 'Ryan didn't exactly scare you and . . .'

Baxter appraised her then flashed a brief smile.

'And you want to know how you can stop Ryan *protecting* you?'

'I do.'

He looked her up and down then did the same to Trip.

'Get a gun.'

'We got guns.'

'Then learn how to use them.'

Baxter pulled his hat down and lifted a leg to mount his horse, but Grace raised a hand and he lowered his leg. His eyes narrowed with a warning that he really did want to leave now.

Grace provided a large and sweet smile.

'I have about all the skill with a gun I'll ever get, and Trip reckons he has enough to take on Ryan, but I don't want him to do that without having an advantage. And I have an idea.' Grace placed her hands on her hips. 'You might like the sound of it.'

CHAPTER 6

'You did what?' Chester shouted, then glanced around the post, ensuring that only Isaac was close. But when he spoke again, he still lowered his voice. 'You've hired a gunslinger to kill Ryan?'

'Not exactly,' Grace said. 'What I reckon—'

'What we reckon . . .' Trip said, interrupting her as he saw from Chester's blazing eyes that he'd never accept an idea if it came from her. He coughed. 'What I reckon is we got to do something while we still got a settlement left.'

Chester turned his irritated gaze on Trip.

'You're just like Milton Calloway, never listening to sense. Not only did you bring bridge workers here to shoot up the place, you then attracted outlaws who demanded money. And now you want to hire a gunslinger to shoot up the outlaws. Where will this end?'

Grace and Trip looked at each other, shaking their heads, but to Trip's surprise, Isaac spoke up.

'Pa,' he said. 'Trip hasn't committed us to hiring this man.'

Chester snorted his breath through his nostrils.

'He hasn't, son,' he snapped, then stamped his boot for emphasis. 'But that doesn't mean I have to listen to this nonsense.'

Isaac shrugged. 'You say I'm old enough to make my own decisions, and if that's true, I'd like to hear his plan.'

'You *are* old enough,' Chester said, waving his hands above his head. 'But age won't bring wisdom if you listen to damn fool ideas like Trip's.'

'I'll listen, but it doesn't mean I have to agree with him. We've always dealt with trouble, but we knew the railroad would bring more people, and people are trouble. If we don't want Ryan to burn Calloway's Crossing to the ground, we need help, and if that means hiring Baxter, then . . . then . . .'

'You'd better not be about to say you support Trip, boy.'

Isaac stood before his father, and Trip guessed that when he'd first offered support for Grace's idea, it'd been guarded, but Chester's belligerent attitude was forcing his son to make a stand. And as that stand probably meant he'd support the idea, Trip kept quiet.

'I do,' Isaac said.

'But . . . But . . . But he wants two hundred dollars. And that's a whole heap of money we just ain't got.'

Isaac frowned. 'I see you've stopped complaining about whether this is the right thing to do, it's just that we can't afford it.'

Chester stabbed a firm finger at Isaac's chest.

'That ain't what I said and you know it.'

'But it is what you mean. You want Ryan to leave, but you got no idea as to how we make him go other than arguing against this idea. So admit it, you like the idea but you're worried about the money.'

'I do not like the idea.' Chester looked away, but a slow sigh slipped from his lips. 'But I guess I hate the idea of parting with two hundred dollars more.'

'And how much trade will we lose with Ryan around?'

Chester closed his eyes and when he spoke, the anger had gone from his voice and his tone was low and defeated.

'I guessed the time when I handed over decisions to you would come one day. Perhaps that day is here already.' He turned to face Isaac and Trip was surprised to detect pride in his eyes after his son had stood up to him. 'How do you propose we raise two hundred dollars, son?'

Isaac lowered his head, breathing deeply as his father acquiesced, and when he looked up he shrugged.

'I don't—'

'I reckon we worry about one thing at a time,' Trip said before Isaac could worry himself into backing down. 'First, we get rid of Ryan. Then, we work out how we pay off Baxter.'

'But that's madness,' Chester said.

'Maybe it is, but I reckon paying off one man once has to be less of a problem than paying off five men every day, surely?'

Within five minutes of agreeing to the plan, Chester

packed the rest of his family off to Wagon Creek to stay out of whatever trouble was about to erupt. Isaac refused to leave and when Trip tentatively suggested that Grace should also leave, she refused his request and instead suggested a refinement to their plan.

Baxter accepted that plan with the briefest of nods then slipped away. Where he went Trip didn't see, but he assumed he was taking up a good position to pull off their plan.

So while Chester prepared the barn, the others headed to the saloon. Inside, Trip strode straight to Ryan's table, set his feet wide, and provided what he hoped would be an honest and resigned smile.

'When do you want your money?' he asked.

'Now would be fine,' Ryan said, as Pike grunted with disappointment. He smiled and leaned back in his chair. 'Then we can leave.'

As Trip nodded, Grace joined them.

'Oh,' she said, lowering her voice to a sultry drawl. 'Do you need to go *now*?'

Ryan shrugged. 'No need to stay once we've been paid.'

'But I thought you might enjoy discussing our arrangements some more.'

'There's nothing to discuss,' Ryan said without taking his gaze away from Trip. 'It's perfectly simple. You pay me fifty dollars every day or Pike burns Calloway's Crossing to the ground.'

'And is that all you want?' she asked.

'All?' Ryan turned to look at Grace. 'What you saying?'

Grace sashayed to Ryan's side. She placed a finger

on his shirt and, just like she'd done when she'd first met Trip, looped it around the cloth and dragged him forward then up from his chair.

'I'm saying we could talk,' she breathed, 'in private – while your men enjoy our beer.'

Ryan glanced down at her bosom then at the finger.

'I got nothing to say that I can't say before my men.'

As everyone grunted their approval, Grace fluffed her hair and lowered her voice to the huskiest of whispers.

'Who said anything about talking?'

'You . . .' A slow grin appeared. 'And where were you thinking of doing this *talking*?'

'The barn.'

Ryan stood back to appraise Grace, then gave a low whistle. As she sidled by him, he barked commands to his men to stay in the saloon, then followed her outside and to the barn, rubbing his hands.

His men swung round to watch them leave, shouting lewd suggestions and joshing Pike about his previous painful encounter with her until they disappeared from view. Then they demanded more beer.

While Isaac served them, Trip mooched around the saloon, feigning indifference, then wandered outside. He closed the door behind him as Ryan and Grace headed into the barn.

Chester was loitering outside the stable where he was out of view from the barn door. Trip gave him a brief nod then hurried to the barn. While Trip had been in the saloon, Chester had pulled his wagon up at the front and Trip jumped on to it, then levered himself up the barn wall to climb in through the open hay barn door. On the upper storey, he collected the gunbelt Chester had placed there then peered down.

Grace and Ryan were standing ten feet in from the door and slightly to the side. Grace had positioned Ryan to face away from the door so that he wouldn't see Trip sneak inside, but so far, she hadn't persuaded him to go to the side so that he'd be below Trip.

'All right,' Ryan was saying. 'Quit the coy saloon-girl act and tell me what you want.'

'That was no act,' Grace said. 'I wanted to get you alone so we could enjoy ourselves a while.'

'And we could, but I'm no fool. I saw what you did to Pike and I know this is just an act. What do you really want?'

'You.'

'Don't believe that,' Ryan snorted and moved to brush by her, but Grace raised a hand, halting him.

'All right. I'll tell you. I want a partnership.'

'Why would that interest me?'

Up in the upper storey of the barn, Trip winced, silently urging Grace to win this debate quickly and get Ryan to the side of the barn. They had planned for Trip to get a drop on him then, with the lead man subdued, to pick off the others one by one using the same tactic of Grace inviting a man to go out into the barn.

The plan would go awry when the remaining men

66

noticed that Ryan hadn't returned. And that was when Baxter would step in. They had several cues, including Grace screaming, for him to appear and join Trip in *persuading* the remaining men to leave, but Trip still hoped they could divide Ryan's forces before they needed Baxter's help.

'It'll interest you,' she said, 'because the railroad's a-coming. You got enough sense to muscle in on it, but you're always moving on. But moving on might not be wise. This area will boom and those with brains and muscle can make plenty. I got the first. You got the second. And I can get us in on schemes you'd never dream of on your own.'

'For example?'

Trip mopped his brow. Grace had reckoned she'd get Ryan to do anything she wanted within seconds of leading him into the barn and neither of them had planned for her sweet-talking to take this long.

In confirmation of the time this was taking, Trip saw a shadow edge out before the barn door and the ever-sceptical Chester shuffled into view, peering into the barn. Ryan and Grace were out of his view and he shuffled another tentative pace.

Trip glared hard at him, hoping that Chester would see him and realize that their plans hadn't gone awry yet, but Chester didn't look up towards the darkened upper story. And he shuffled another pace.

Grace arched her back, possibly masking a wince as she saw Chester's shadow appear around the barn door, then pointed to the side of the barn.

'I was standing up all last night and I'm not used to that. Perhaps we could sit down over there and discuss my ideas – and without the coy saloon-girl act.'

Ryan nodded and took a pace to the side. Grace heaved a sigh of relief and glanced towards Trip's position, who kept completely still.

But outside, Chester still couldn't see either of them and they were moving even further away from his line of sight. He edged another short pace closer to the barn door.

On the upper storey, Trip stood as Ryan disappeared from his view then slipped to the edge, ready to get a drop on him, but then Chester darted his head forwards to peer around the side of the door. He put a hand to his brow as he peered around the darkened interior.

'What the—?' Ryan murmured, striding back into Trip's view and glaring at Chester.

Trip darted back to avoid Ryan seeing him, but his sudden movement dragged a creak from the wood beneath his feet making Ryan do a double-take then glance up. He flinched as he saw Trip wavering close to the edge.

Trip rocked from foot to foot, but then accepted he had no choice but to act. He took a long pace forwards and leapt from the upper storey, aiming to bundle Ryan to the ground. But with Ryan already alerted, his target jumped aside and Trip hit the ground heavily on his feet, then tumbled to his knees before sprawling on to his chest, winded.

On the ground, Trip shook himself, pain numbing his knees and feet, then rolled on to his back, but it was to stare up into the barrel of Ryan's drawn gun.

He had a firm hand clamped on Grace's arm and Chester was loitering by the barn door with his hands thrust high.

With a short twitch of his gun, Ryan signified that he should get up and, while clutching his chest, Trip stood, exaggerating his hurt as he swayed on the spot.

Ryan signified that Trip should walk ahead of him and with Ryan at the back, the group left the barn.

In the doorway, Trip stopped for long enough to flash an annoyed glare at Chester, but Ryan kicked him forward then sighted Chester down the barrel of his gun. Chester cringed away as Ryan fired, but the shot only winged his hat to the ground.

'Any more tricks,' Ryan said, 'and somebody will pay in blood.'

Chester retrieved his hat as the gunfire enticed Ryan's men to come outside. They emerged sporting the grins and good-natured airs of people who had enjoyed too much beer that afternoon, but that attitude died as soon as they saw Ryan holding Chester and the others at gunpoint.

They ripped out their guns. Heath walked sideways to the barn, glancing around, while the other men spread out.

'No need to do nothing,' Trip said. 'We'll pay. I got your fifty dollars.'

Ryan snorted. 'Fifty is what I wanted before you tried that trick. Now I want one hundred, every day.'

'We can't pay that much.'

Ryan took a long pace towards Trip, his eyes blazing, but Grace screeched. Without taking his gaze from Trip, Ryan released his grip of her arm then swung up his left hand, clipping her around the back of the head and knocking her to the ground. But when she hit the ground, she rolled to her knees then threw back her head and screamed, the sound echoing back and forth between the buildings in Calloway's Crossing.

Ryan stared down at her, but her screaming continued unabated as if her lungs would never give out.

'Finished?' he asked when she'd delivered her last warbling screech.

'You're not going to . . . going to . . . kill him, are you?' she babbled, her eyes wide and scared. Then she thrust a knuckle to her mouth and bit it.

Ryan stared at her, his brow furrowed, then shrugged and looked at Trip, who had used the distraction to back away several paces, then at Chester who was darting his gaze in all directions. He flinched.

'Wait! What's happening here?'

'Nothing,' Trip said. From the corner of his eye, he noticed that Chester was still glancing around. And the hobbling Pike had dragged Isaac from the saloon and he was edging from foot to foot.

'That ain't right. You're all acting strange.'

Trip's throat went dry, but he avoided the urge to gulp.

'We're just scared.'

'You *are* scared, but I've seen plenty of scared people, and you ain't acting like them. You're expecting something to happen.' Ryan glanced around. 'What is it?'

Ryan was right. By now, Baxter should have emerged from wherever he was hiding and be making Ryan pay with hot lead, but as yet, he hadn't showed.

Trip spread his hands and joined Ryan in glancing around Calloway's Crossing, still seeing no sign of Baxter's impending help.

'I don't know,' he said with all honesty. 'I just don't know.'

CHAPTER 7

'Where is he?' Trip whispered.

'No idea,' Grace said from the corner of her mouth. 'But his horse's gone. We've got to hope Ryan doesn't realize what we tried to do or none of us will get out of here alive.'

The last ten minutes had been fraught.

Ryan had searched everyone, confiscating every gun, then herded them into the saloon. He'd positioned them in the centre of the room while he conferred with his men by the door. And their low tones and frequent glances their way suggested they'd decided that something was wrong, but they didn't know what it was.

'Then,' Trip said, 'we got to come up with another plan.'

'I know, but I can't—'

'Be quiet,' Ryan shouted, striding across the saloon to confront them. 'I've had enough of your scheming.'

'We were discussing how we'd pay you,' Trip said, presenting Ryan with a wide smile. 'I'll fetch your money now, if you want.'

Ryan eyed Trip with suspicion. 'I'm no fool. You're not leaving to try another scheme. Nobody leaves until I have one hundred dollars. Give it to me now or someone dies.' Ryan roved his gun in a sweeping arc, taking in Chester, Isaac, Trip and stopping at Grace. 'And that someone will be you.'

As Grace produced an audible gulp and Pike gibbered with barely suppressed glee, Trip glanced at Isaac and Chester, who both returned nervous and silent pleas for him to do something. He looked out the window, seeing no sign of anyone approaching or any hint that Baxter had done anything but abandon them.

He sighed as he considered how much money he'd made last night and, although he'd earmarked most of it for buying new stock and repairing the broken furniture, he accepted he'd have to give it to Ryan.

'All right,' he said. 'I can cover the one hundred dollars. It doesn't leave me anything to—'

'That ain't my problem,' Ryan grunted. 'The money, now.'

Trip pointed. 'It's behind the bar.'

Ryan ordered Pike to collect it and Pike shuffled away, his eyes downcast and disappointed. He bent to look over the bar, but at that moment, Trip saw metal glint then a gun emerge from under the bar. The barrel slammed under Pike's chin.

Trip saw a hand and arm emerge and he just had time to realize that Baxter had been hiding there all along. Then the gun roared, knocking Pike's head back so that he stood straight before he tumbled away with his arms splayed. Even before he'd hit the floor, Baxter rose from behind the bar – a guntoting avenger with twin guns brandished and spewing lead.

Ryan and his men swirled round to face him, scrambling for their guns, but before they could fire a single shot, Baxter's guns belched fire in four crisp and neat shots.

The first two bullets scythed through two of Ryan's men, taking them with high shots to the sides of the head that spun them away. The third tore through the next man's neck, wheeling him over.

Only the shot that sliced a furrow across Ryan's cheek was non-fatal, but any hint that that was a mistake fled when Baxter fired again, winging Ryan's gun from his hand.

The force swung Ryan round, but he rocked back, wringing his hand, to face a man who had fixed him with his firm gaze and even firmer guns.

Baxter paced out from behind the bar, showing no sign of his apparent lethargy as he walked sideways with his guns never straying from Ryan.

'You ready to beg for your life?' Nothing in Baxter's hollow tone suggested his request was open to negotiation.

Ryan gulped. 'Maybe we can—'

Baxter's guns blasted lead, both shots slamming straight between Ryan's eyes, rocking his head back to stand him straight before he tumbled backwards like a felled tree.

Baxter twirled one gun back into his holster. The

other disappeared with a shrug, perhaps up his sleeve, then he took several long paces to walk over Ryan's body.

Nobody made a sound as he headed to the door, but he stopped in the doorway and spoke while still looking outside.

'I'll dispose of the horses,' he said. 'You clean up the mess.'

And with that, he left them.

Ten minutes after Baxter's sudden appearance, everyone had calmed sufficiently to act on his instructions.

But first, Chester and Isaac danced a celebratory jig and, unlike the previous time, Trip clapped his hands as they whirled, and when Grace held out an arm, he even did a few reels with her.

Then they set about cleaning up the saloon. With Chester having sent the rest of his family away, they had to do all the work themselves, but it didn't take them long to drag the bodies outside to Chester's wagon.

The saloon floor was dirt and the fighting the night before had produced several sticky patches of blood so that the extra stains produced by the gunfight didn't appear anomalous. Even so, several buckets of water from the river cleaned away all signs of what had happened.

And when Trip emerged from the saloon, Grace was standing on the back of the wagon with the bodies lined up at her feet.

'Look what I've found,' she shouted, holding open Ryan's jacket.

Trip hurried over and, with Chester, rolled onto the back of the wagon to hunker down beside Ryan's body. Trip saw the envelope in her hand and the bills poking out.

'How much?' Chester asked, his eyes gleaming.

Grace fingered through the bills then waggled her eyebrows.

'At least fifty dollars. And that isn't all.' She patted Ryan's pocket then withdrew a silver watch. 'This has to be worth plenty, too.'

'Yeah,' Chester grumbled, 'to the person he stole it off.'

Grace looked around. 'Don't see that person here now.'

'That may be your way, but it ain't mine. If these men stole property, we will return it.'

Grace sighed as she hefted the watch. 'No way of knowing where the money came from, though.'

Chester glanced at Trip, who returned an encouraging nod.

'All right. We'll keep the money but not anything we can trace back to someone.'

'Then we're fine here.' Grace dangled the watch on the end of its chain and swung it back and forth, the sun reflecting a bead of light across Chester's face. 'There's no inscription and no way of knowing where it came from. What do you think of that?'

Chester closed his eyes and murmured to himself.

'Have you searched the other bodies?' he asked.

Grace whooped, then shuffled down the line of bodies to carry out a thorough search while Trip headed off to riffle through the saddle-bags that

Baxter had discarded before he led the horses away.

Fifteen minutes later, they congregated in the saloon. On the bar was the heap of their findings. And it represented a fine haul with Trip's initial totting up of the windfall being more than two hundred dollars.

Every body had money on it, although not as much as the fifty dollars that Ryan had on him. And even if they were to hide the stolen trinkets for a prudent amount of time then sell them cheaply, Trip estimated that they could pay off Baxter and clear thirty dollars apiece.

'Now,' Isaac said, looking at his father, 'who says I was wrong to support Trip's idea?'

Chester considered the pile of dollars then shook his head.

'I do. No matter what the result, it was wrong to get those men killed. Never forget that.'

'And?'

Chester sighed. 'And I guess I'm glad they're dead and I'm not disappointed that this didn't go worse than it could have done.'

As Isaac continued to look at his father, presumably hoping for more words of encouragement, Trip raised a hand.

'That's enough talk,' he said. 'We got to make sure nobody can work out what happened here.' He looked at each person in turn. 'Not ever.'

Everybody provided sombre nods and, without another word, Isaac and Chester hurried outside to complete the cleaning up, while Trip and Grace went to the wagon. At a steady pace, they headed out of town and into the wood that started a mile down-river.

Grace pulled up at a secluded spot and when they'd unloaded the bodies, Trip reckoned they should bury them, but she overruled him. So they dragged the bodies into a dense thicket and arranged them so that it looked like they'd been ambushed and met their fate there.

Grace reckoned scavengers would find them soon and, if anyone were to happen across whatever they left behind, the scene would present a less suspicious discovery than if anyone were to find shallow graves.

When they returned to Calloway's Crossing, Chester had liberally dosed the area between the buildings with water, removing any sign that anyone had ever visited the settlement. Isaac had scrubbed the bar and table in the saloon and was making a bonfire of the broken furniture outside.

Trip had hoped to repair some of that furniture, but he kept his irritation to himself and, with Grace, headed into the saloon. They put aside two hundred dollars to pay Baxter and divided up the remaining money and possessions.

Then Chester and Isaac joined them and sitting around the table they concocted an alternate story of Ryan's visit to Calloway's Crossing, which they'd relate if anyone ever found the bodies or came looking for Ryan. But as they were finalizing the details, Trip heard a rider pull up outside.

Trip ran behind the bar and swept the windfall to the floor, then swung round to face the door while sporting an innocent smile. But the door opened to reveal Baxter, standing with his blanket thrown over a shoulder.

Trip breathed a sigh of relief then beckoned him to come to the bar.

'Horses gone,' Baxter confirmed. He glanced around the post then rubbed a boot over the wet floor, nodding.

'And we've all agreed that nothing happened here,' Trip said. 'If you know what I mean.'

'I do.'

'And now you'll be leaving?' Trip watched Baxter provide a slow nod then rummaged beneath the bar. He placed a pile of bills on the bar and pushed them towards him.

Baxter looked at the bills, his brow furrowing, then joined Trip. He counted the bills then raised his blanket to slot the wad into a pocket.

'I ain't heading back this way. Be obliged if you'd pay me in full.'

'We agreed on two hundred,' Trip intoned. He gave a pronounced gulp, the action not helping to moisten his dry throat as Chester jumped up from the table to glare at him.

'We did.' Baxter fixed Trip with his piercing gaze. 'But I didn't just run Ryan out of town. I killed him.'

'But . . . But . . .'

Chester joined them and raised a hand. 'Quit leading us on and tell us what you want.'

'For killing five men I don't want two hundred dollars.' Baxter turned and headed back across the saloon. 'I want two thousand dollars.'

'You can't be serious,' Trip blurted after him.

Baxter stopped a moment then continued his pacing across the room. Without looking at any of them, he lay down, unfurled his blanket, pulled it up to his chin, then drew his hat down over his eyes. But Trip saw the bulge under the blanket and knew that his gun rested on his chest.

Baxter raised the hat and opened an eye.

'You'll want to talk about this outside,' he said, then drew the hat back down.

Chester glared hard at Trip, but Trip did as suggested and led everyone outside. They wandered round the side of the saloon to stand beside the dry gully. The mound of earth the burrowing animal was creating had grown again and more fresh earth was strewn down the bank.

Trip sat on the top of the mound considering the dirt, with Isaac and Chester flanking him. Grace stayed back against the wall.

'Didn't you agree terms with him?' Chester muttered.

'Yeah.' Trip kicked at the loose earth at his feet. 'Two hundred dollars for getting rid of Ryan.'

'But did you agree he'd have to kill him?'

Trip looked at Grace, who shrugged.

'That doesn't matter,' she said. 'We have to stop arguing and decide what we do now.'

'And we do nothing,' Chester said. 'You saw the way he shoots. He's a lightning-fast draw and none of us can take him on.'

Trip shook his head. 'No matter how fast a man is, he can't do nothing when he's surrounded. There's four of us and if we—'

'We won't do that.' Chester waved in a dismissive manner at him then turned to Isaac. 'See what happens, boy, when you listen to men like Trip?'

'I guess I do,' Isaac murmured, lowering his head.

Chester waggled a finger. 'Then let that be a valuable lesson for you. And here comes another one. We're in deep trouble, but there's no need for us to go any deeper.'

Chester beckoned for Isaac to join him then headed to the barn with Grace and Trip trailing behind.

'You can't ignore this,' Trip said. 'We have to work together.'

Chester snorted but didn't stop his determined pacing.

'And you're suggesting we take this gunslinger on, are you? Presumably with the help of an even faster gunslinger who'll demand even more money?'

'No. It seems I agreed to pay Baxter two thousand dollars and as we ain't got that sort of money, we have to face him down.'

He glanced at Grace and she murmured her support, but neither Isaac nor Chester slowed their pace.

'No we don't. And you just provided the answer. *You* agreed to pay him that money.' Chester stopped beside his wagon to glare at Trip. 'It's got nothing to do with me.'

Chester slapped his son's shoulder then jumped up on to his wagon.

'You can't walk away from this,' Trip said, exchanging an incredulous glance with Grace.

'We are and we will,' Chester said, rolling into the seat. 'I said I'd make you suffer for threatening to blow up my dam. I reckon I'm doing that.'

'I agree with Pa,' Isaac said, flopping onto the seat beside Chester. 'If Baxter wants two thousand dollars, he'll have to find us first.'

'My son speaks plenty of sense,' Chester said. 'And I reckon you got yourself a choice. Sort out your problem, or do the same as we're doing.'

'And what's that?'

Chester raised the reins. 'Run and hide.'

'You can't really intend to—' Trip swung away, throwing an arm to his face to avoid the grit flying up from the wheels.

When Trip swung back, the wagon was hurtling down the trail and within two minutes, the cloud of dust from Chester's wagon had blown away. And Chester and Isaac were just distant and shrinking blots on the horizon.

Ten minutes later, Trip headed into the saloon.

'We haven't got two thousand dollars,' he said. He set his feet wide and stared down at Baxter's form, his face hidden by his hat and the blanket pulled up to his chin. 'So we either deal with this in here or outside.'

'No need to get yourself killed now that Chester's gone.' Baxter raised his hat with a finger and provided a sly smile.

'Only person in danger here is you.'

Baxter ran his gaze from Trip's face down to his hip to consider the holstered gun and the hand dangling beside it.

'Men who talk like that don't talk again.' Baxter shrugged. 'Same goes for womenfolk.'

'It's just between us two.'

Baxter snorted a laugh. 'Grace has a rifle aimed at the back of my head. You reckon that's enough to take me. You're wrong.'

'And you've got a cocked gun under that blanket. You might take me, but one way or the other you *will* die under that blanket unless you take the two hundred dollars we agreed on and leave town.'

Baxter bored his gaze into Trip then delivered a slow nod.

'You got the guts to go for your gun, but Grace hasn't. She'll hesitate and that'll give me the time to take you both.'

Trip firmed his jaw, but couldn't help but dart his gaze to the wall where Grace had slipped a rifle through a tear in the cloth from outside. When he looked back, Baxter was smiling, confirming that his mistake had revealed Grace's exact location.

'You may be right, but do you want to take the risk when there ain't no way we can ever pay you two thousand dollars?' Trip raised his hands, signifying that Baxter should look around the saloon. 'Look at this place. Would it be in this state if we had that much money?

'You're right, but you see, the thing about being asleep is you hear things people wouldn't say when you're awake.' Baxter raised his eyebrows. 'I know how you can pay me off.'

Trip shook his head and inched his hand towards

his holster, but as Baxter narrowed his eyes, Grace paced through the long tear in the wall and headed across the saloon. When she'd walked into Baxter's line of sight, she stopped and raised the rifle.

'What do you want us to do?' she asked.

'You sure about this?' Trip asked.

Grace drew her horse to a halt by the side of the river. Towering ahead were the struts of the bridge across Calloway's Gulch, the framework now nearing completion. The workers were building the top layer and several lengths of wood had stretched all the way across.

'Nope,' she said, 'but have you had a better idea yet?'

'I haven't, but ever since you got us into this—'

'Trip Kincaid, I thought you were man enough not to mention it was my idea to hire Baxter.'

'But it was.'

'And you thought it was a good idea right up until the moment—'

'Until the moment Baxter made us become outlaws.'

'He hasn't made us do that exactly and besides, your idea of taking him on would have got us both killed, wouldn't it?' Grace watched Trip nod. 'So keep your opinions to yourself and let me do the thinking from now on.'

Trip opened his mouth to offer an opinion about what her thinking had led them to, then thought better of it. But he was still shaking his head as they headed into Calloway's Gulch where several men broke off from working to greet their arrival with friendly waves, most directed at Grace.

They returned the waves and joined them to exchange pleasantries while Trip searched for an excuse that would let them stay without raising suspicions. In truth, they had no good reason for being here, but just as Trip was feeling that his animated talk was appearing false, Frank Moore emerged from the shack he'd erected overlooking the bridge and hailed them.

'Howdy, Trip,' he said. 'I was hoping I'd see you. Have you seen Ryan Trimble? He headed off to your saloon and nobody has seen him since.'

'He left,' Trip said, gritting his teeth to avoid showing surprise. 'He didn't say where he was going.'

Frank sighed. 'I know he's caused you trouble and you don't care what he does, but I need him.' He lowered his voice. 'The money's due at first light tomorrow.'

Trip glanced at Grace, seeing in her blank expression the fact that she was letting him carry on pumping Frank for information.

Their instructions were to learn as much as possible about the delivery tomorrow then report their findings to Baxter. Trip had brought a bottle of whiskey as an excuse to stay, and Grace had planned to talk Frank round to revealing that information when he was suitably relaxed. But Frank had revealed the most crucial detail without prompting.

Trip offered to open the bottle. Frank didn't want a drink, but neither did he send them away, seemingly enjoying having someone around with whom

85

he could unburden his woes.

So Grace and Trip sat outside the shack and encouraged him to talk, while repeatedly glancing down the trail as if they were also awaiting Ryan's arrival.

Periodically, workers whom Frank had sent off to search for him returned, shaking their heads, and each time Grace and Trip provided woeful expressions. Curiously, the man who had headed off to find out whether Adam Calloway had seen him reported that Adam was nowhere to be found either.

But amidst the woe, piece by piece, Frank revealed the details of tomorrow's schedule.

At first light, ten blue coats – the guards who delivered the railroad payroll – would arrive. They'd leave twenty thousand dollars in a compact strongbox. Two thousand was to pay the workers and the rest was for Adam Calloway. Adam would take the money as soon as it arrived, but the workers wouldn't get their wages until they'd finished work for the day.

But Frank had no contingency plans to guard the money if Ryan didn't return. The sun was casting long shadows of the bridge across the gulch when he ran out of problems to complain about and returned to a sullen consideration of the trail.

As staying to await a man who wouldn't return ran the danger of appearing suspicious, Trip and Grace bade Frank farewell and left him. They rode off, but when they were out of view from the bridge, they circled back and headed up the side of the bluff to Adam Calloway's shack.

Adam still hadn't returned, so they leaned back

against the front of his building in a position where they could look down on the bridge and see most of the activity that was taking place below.

Trip shuffled from side to side as, through the tops of the trees, he watched the distant form of Frank Moore pace back and forth. Periodically, Frank broke off to speak to his men when they returned, then resumed pacing, that pacing becoming more fevered as the sun closed on the horizon.

At sundown, the bridge workers filed away from their work and settled down to eat, but still Frank didn't join them and paced on.

'What's so worrying?' Grace asked.

'He must be real worried that someone will steal the money.'

'Perhaps he is, but I didn't mean him. You're pacing around as much as Frank is. Relax. All this will be over soon.'

'I know, but I can't wait to get back to running a saloon and not having to deal with Chester and outlaws and gunslingers.' Trip paced back and forth once more then took Grace's suggestion and joined her. He leaned back against the wall beside her.

'And then our real worries start,' she mused. 'What I said to Ryan in the barn was right. The railroad *will* change everything. Calloway's Crossing will make money for the next month, but when the railroad moves on, there'll be no need for such a place outside Wagon Creek. Why else would Chester so readily abandon his business?'

Trip sighed. 'Because it wasn't worth fighting for?'

'It wasn't.' Grace raised her eyebrows. 'But with a

small investment, we could open a proper saloon in Wagon Creek that would make real money.'

Trip nodded. 'A good idea, but we have to pay off Baxter first.'

'You have,' a voice intoned from beside the building.

Trip flinched then turned to see Baxter emerge from the gloom.

'How long have you been there?' Trip asked.

'Long enough to also wonder why Frank's so nervous.' Baxter joined them and leaned back against the wall with a foot raised and the sole of his boot pressed flat to the wall. 'What did you learn?'

Trip relayed the information they'd gathered. Throughout, Baxter remained silent, speaking only at the end to check through the details using his usual terse tone. Then he pushed himself from the wall and headed to the corner of the building.

'Keep watch tonight,' he ordered. 'If anything happens, tell me.'

'How will we find you?' Trip shouted after him.

Baxter stopped a moment then headed past the corner of the building.

'Don't worry,' he said, as he melted into the gathering gloom. 'I'll find you.'

CHAPTER 8

Night gathered leaving the only light source as the half-moon that scudded in and out of high cloud. As neither Trip nor Grace had thought they'd be keeping vigil all night, they hadn't brought along anything to eat, and they only had the whiskey to drink.

As the workers below settled down to an early sleep and the half-moon edged towards the horizon, the night chill gathered around them. They didn't dare light a fire, so they opened the bottle.

An hour later, a pleasant lethargy was overcoming the boredom and the worry of being involved in an attempt to steal twenty thousand dollars from the railroad.

'What we waiting for?' Grace said, her voice slurring as she peered at the whiskey sloshing in the bottom of the bottle, then covered a polite hiccup with her hand.

'We are waiting for anything unusual,' Trip said, taking the bottle from her. He watched Grace shuffle to her feet and lurch a few paces towards the edge of the bluff to look down. He laughed. 'You not drink whiskey that often?'

'Only to satisfy my customers, but I got no need to let liquor dull my life.' She shrugged, the action knocking her back a pace. 'Not yet, anyhow.'

'You not enjoy what you do?'

'It's all right, but there has to . . .' She considered him then paced towards him and flopped down on to her knees. 'But enough of me. How do you reckon we pass the time after we've drunk the whiskey?'

Trip took a deep breath of cooling night air, noticing that on an empty stomach he was more light-headed than he expected.

He shrugged. 'We got our orders. We keep watch.'

Grace smiled, her teeth dazzling in the gloom as she leaned towards him and breathed pleasant whiskey fumes over him.

'I reckon we'd already established we're keeping watch.' She leaned a mite closer, the action making her right arm give way so that she tumbled to her elbows. She snapped back up but still leaned in to him with an errant lock of hair now dangling over her face. 'I meant what are we going to do *while* we keep watch?'

'Can't think of anything.'

She snorted then shuffled round on her haunches to sit beside him, but her foot slipped from under her and she stumbled into him. She moved to get up, but then sighed and leaned her head on his shoulder.

'You haven't got much of an imagination, have you, Trip Kincaid?' she mused, her voice light and wistful.

'Ain't had much need for one.' He considered. 'Guess we could talk.'

'Talk!' She raised her head to look at him then chuckled. 'You sure aren't like any man I've ever met before.'

'How so?'

'What am I right now?'

Trip leaned back to consider her. 'This some kind of guessing game?'

'No.' She slapped his arm then took the bottle from him. She raised it to her lips then hiccuped and returned it to him without drinking.

'I reckon one answer is that you're a little drunk.'

'Right, but not the answer I wanted.' She fluffed at her hair then tucked the errant lock of hair behind her ear. 'What do I do?'

'You're a . . . a saloon-girl.'

She nodded vigorously, freeing the tangle of hair again.

'And how long have we known each other?'

'Six, seven days.'

'And most men don't go six, seven minutes before they're inviting me to . . . to get to know them better, but you haven't done that and not even when I'm a little bit . . .' She held out a shaking hand. 'A little bit . . .'

'A little bit what?'

She moistened her lips. 'A little bit suggestible as to what we could be doing while we keep watch.'

Trip couldn't help but gulp. 'Then you're right. I'm not like those other men. I wouldn't take no advantage of no woman when she'd had whiskey on an empty stomach.'

Her eyes widened as she snorted her breath.

'*You* take advantage of *me*. Now let me tell you something, Trip Kincaid, I—' She flinched then swirled round to peer into the darkness. 'Did you hear that?'

Trip heard rustling, as of someone or something pushing through the trees and approaching the house.

'Animal?'

'Animals hear you, not you hear them.'

'Baxter?'

'Same.'

'Then someone from the bridge coming to look for Adam?'

'Or Adam himself, or perhaps someone hearing us making noise and coming to investigate.'

'Either way, us being here looks mighty suspicious. We got to hide.'

'Too late,' Grace said, as the masked glow of a brand appeared through the trees, the glow already enlightening the side of the building as the holder approached.

'Then think up an excuse for us being here.'

Grace nodded. 'I have a good one.'

'Then tell me what it is,' Trip murmured, as the glow from the approaching brand spread out to light Grace's wicked smile.

'It doesn't involve words. It'd be quicker if I just showed you.'

'Then do it quickly before—'

Trip didn't get to complete his order as Grace

looped an arm around his neck and dragged him backwards.

Trip struggled for a moment, but by then he was lying flat on his back and Grace was lying on top of him.

And by the time the approaching man stopped twenty yards from the building and had them in full sight, Ryan Trimble's ghost could have paraded around him with a loaded Peacemaker and he'd have still ignored him.

The heavy morning clouds were lifting with the promise of a warm day when Trip shuffled to the doorway to look outside. The river's soft gurgling drifted to him on the morning breeze.

Grace joined him at the door. 'What you thinking?' she asked.

'Nothing. Just enjoying watching the day get started.'

'It's already done that.' Grace stretched. 'And what will it bring?'

Trip looked towards the bridge.

'Got no idea, but I hope it's better than yesterday.'

She slapped his arm. 'You not enjoy last night?'

'I did, but . . .'

'Then you're not worrying that you took advantage of me or some other damn fool notion, are you, Trip Kincaid?' She kneaded her forehead and clapped her mouth. 'Although I won't hurry to drink our whiskey again.'

'I wasn't worrying about that, but I did want to ask you about . . .' Trip glanced at her then returned to looking outside. He sighed and lowered his voice. 'About what we did last night after we broke in here and . . . and about whether it means we'll do it again.'

Grace smiled then looped an arm in his. 'We might do it again sometime, if that's what you mean.'

'It wasn't exactly,' Trip murmured. 'I was wondering . . .'

She flinched away then paced out through the door to stand outside.

'Why is it always the same? You have some fun with a man. Then he spoils it all by getting serious.' She swirled round and faced him with her hands on hips. 'I'm a saloon-girl. I earn a living by doing what we did last night. But that's work and sometimes I fancy playing a little, understand?'

'I know what you used to do, but I thought you wouldn't do that again unless you . . .' Trip sighed. 'I just hoped you'd want something more.'

'Nothing more, Trip Kincaid, nothing more. I got a living to earn.'

Trip slapped the side of the doorframe.

'Then find another way, something that doesn't—'

'Something that doesn't let men paw and grope me? Something that'll let me keep my dignity?'

'If you got to put it like that, yeah.'

'But I keep that. It's the men who lose their dignity, and their money. And while they've busy making fools of themselves, I learn plenty about them. Take Adam Calloway, for instance. He's a man who I wouldn't expect to go missing and yet—'

'You've been with Adam?'

'Yeah.'

'And many of the other men around here?'

'To name the ones you know, Adam and Milton and Marshal—'

'Enough,' Trip shouted, slapping his hands over his ears. 'I don't want to know, and I don't want to know what you learnt about me last night either.'

'I wasn't looking to learn anything. I was enjoying myself and before you go and get a mind to get all serious again, Trip Kincaid, remember that.'

Trip whistled through his teeth. 'You ain't like any woman I've ever met.'

'And you aren't like any man I've ever met. So let's keep it like that.' Grace padded away to stand on the edge of the bluff then coughed and gestured over her shoulder. 'Trip, you got to come and see this.'

Trip pushed himself from the door and headed over to see what had concerned her. When he joined her, he could see down onto the bridge site. Mayhem had broken out with people running in all directions, their cries carrying up to him on the morning breeze and they didn't sound happy.

'The money?'

Grace glanced to the east. Dense clouds still obscured the sun, but a focus of light was high in the sky, suggesting it was mid-morning.

'I reckon we slept in too long. Baxter's already stolen it.'

Trip watched the bridge workers mill for a few more minutes, but although he still couldn't see what was concerning them, he had to agree that this was the most likely explanation.

95

So they headed down to the bridge and quickly confirmed that Grace's assumption was correct. In fact, Frank was already organizing a quest to reclaim the money, but despite the chaos, Trip couldn't see any sign of anyone having been killed or injured. So Baxter must have accomplished his raid in a bloodless manner that Trip hadn't expected.

They reached the bridge as two groups of men headed off in different directions, one upriver and in the general direction of Calloway's Crossing, and the other towards Wagon Creek.

This left around a dozen men at the gulch, including Frank, who, as silence returned, hailed them.

'What's happened? Trip asked, riding up to him.

'The money's gone,' Frank wailed, wringing his hands, 'that's what's happened.'

'See who stole it?'

'No. Just after the blue coats had left, this strut on the bridge fell into the river. I organized the men to stop the whole bridge falling down, but it was a distraction and somebody stole the money.'

Trip dismounted and provided a sympathetic smile.

'Any idea who the raiders were?'

'No.' Frank considered Trip. 'Did you see anything from up there?'

'Nothing.'

Frank turned away, but then swung back.

'And why were you up at Adam's place last night?'

'Well,' Trip said, coughing and having no trouble in appearing sheepish. 'We don't like to say.'

'Yeah, I heard about what you were doing, but you

didn't need to come all the way out here to do that.'

Trip considered Frank's firm jaw and the veneer of accusation that was overcoming his eyes and tone. He lowered his voice.

'We had nothing to do with the raid if that's what you're suggesting.'

'I don't know what I'm suggesting, but yesterday you asked a whole heap of questions about the arrangements for today, and you spent the night here.' Frank glanced at Grace then at their horses then at Trip's saddle-bag, which contained only the empty bottle of whiskey. 'You mind if I search you?'

'I don't reckon . . .' Trip sighed, accepting that their actions did appear suspicious and that allaying those suspicions was the only way they could move on quickly. 'Go on. We got nothing to hide.'

Frank gestured for one of the workers to frisk them, then stood back. He eyed them with continued suspicion, but when the man confirmed that Trip wasn't hiding anything and moved on to Grace, he relaxed his shoulders.

'Sorry about this,' he said. 'I guess I'm jumpy. I'm suspecting everyone now.'

'Don't worry about it. I'd probably do the same in your position. As soon as this is over, we'll help you track down who did it.'

Frank nodded as the man finished searching Grace and turned to their horses.

Grace glanced at Trip with a wide-eyed look, which asked whether his offer was serious, and Trip returned a wink, which said they could look but they didn't have to find anybody.

'Obliged,' Frank said. 'I need all the help I can—'

'What's this?' the man muttered behind Trip and Trip turned to see him holding his saddle-bag high. Clutched in his other hand was a large folded wad of bills.

And Trip reckoned there had to be at least a thousand dollars there.

CHAPTER 9

'That's not what it looks like,' Trip murmured, staring at the wad of bills. 'Someone's planted that money.'

'They didn't,' Frank snorted. 'That's your cut for keeping lookout.'

Trip gulped, his guts churning with the fact that Frank's guess could be right. He hadn't figured that Baxter would leave him with anything, but maybe he had.

Frank advanced on Trip. Behind him, the workers who were still at the bridge were eyeing developments with interest as they paced in towards Trip.

'I got no idea what's happened here,' Trip said, backing away a pace towards his horse.

'The railroad won't deliver another payroll, so we've all worked for nothing.' Frank gestured at his advancing men. 'You want to explain to us how sorry you are?'

Trip gulped as he looked around the approaching arc of men and none of them appeared ready to listen to an explanation as they moved purposefully towards him, rolling their shoulders. He backed away another pace, but one man lunged in and grabbed his arms, and another lunged for his gun and tossed it to the ground.

'You can't blame us,' Trip said.

'I'm not blaming *her*. You just paid her to keep you company last night. But I am blaming you.'

'Then I'm glad we got that cleared up.'

Trip went limp then threw out his arms, knocking the man holding him away, and turned towards his horse, but two men paced round to stand between him and his steed. Trip still broke into a run and headed straight for them.

They closed ranks with two other men joining him to block his route, but at the last moment Trip dug a heel in, skidded to a halt, then ran off in the opposite direction towards the bridge.

'Get him!' Frank shouted, but Trip thrust his head forward and pumped his arms as he ran as fast he could.

He glanced over his shoulder to confirm Frank's men were only holding Grace and not accosting her, then swirled round and concentrated on running. The first slim planks now stretched across the gulch and, in a less desperate situation than he was in, he would have headed across them. But he judged that the workers had more skill at balancing than he had and veered to the side.

He headed upriver towards Calloway's Crossing. The workers had cleared trees for several hundred yards around the bridge and he aimed to get into the wood then lose his pursuers in the dense undergrowth.

But before he'd even halved the distance, hoofs pounded behind him. He glanced back to see that three of the workers had hurried to their horses and were galloping after him. And they swirled lassos over their heads as they swooped in at him from three different directions.

Men were chasing on foot behind them, but the riders were only thirty yards away and would cut him off within seconds and long before he reached the trees. Still, Trip ran on, hoping he might get lucky, as the hoofs pounded closer and closer until he heard the swirl of rope whistle through the air. He dropped his head, the lasso closing on air as the first pursuer galloped by.

Trip dug in a heel then did an abrupt right turn and headed for the river.

The rider who had surged by him pulled back on the reins then closed in on him again, and the other two riders swooped in. The men on foot milled around them, closing off Trip's escape routes in case he kept out of the riders' clutches.

The next rider hurled his lasso and again Trip flinched out of the way, but the third man had him in his sights and bore down on him. The rope swirled straight for Trip's head. He threw himself to the ground, rolling over a shoulder, and the rope missed his head, but caught a trailing foot and dragged him to a grinding halt.

On his back, he grabbed his foot and peeled the rope away, before the rider could take advantage of the situation, and came back up on his feet and began running for the river. Now he was just fifty

yards from the slope down to the river, the trees 200
yards to his side and impossible to reach.

Behind him, the riders and men chased him, and
Trip reckoned they would intercept him before he
reached the slope. But even with his breath coming
in harsh gasps as he failed to gain more speed, they
didn't close.

Trip enjoyed a moment of elation before he realized they were letting him reach the river. There, all
escape routes ended. He ran to the edge of the slope,
paused to look back and see the mass of men were
still around twenty yards back, then hurried down
the side.

Several hundreds yards away from the bridge, the
slope wasn't so steep but the sides were crumbling so
that Trip had to fight to keep his balance, leaning
back as he waded downwards through the shifting
dirt.

Behind him, the men fanned out, slowing to
ensure he couldn't head to the gulch or to the trees.
So when Trip stomped to a halt before the river, he
had a few moments to search for a way out before
they advanced on him.

As the river had appeared negotiable from on
high, on the way down he'd entertained the thought
of jumping into the water. But closer to, he saw that
it had none of the gurgling pleasantness of
Calloway's Crossing. Here, the narrow sides
converted the river into a roaring, swirling mass
filled with boulders and white-foamed breakwaters
that'd drag a man under in seconds.

He swirled round then glanced up, confirming

that Grace hadn't been able to follow him, then faced the approaching mass of men.

The men paced in and surrounded him, even cutting him off from the river. Frank stood before him, but Trip didn't meet his eye, preferring to look at the other men and to try to convince them he was innocent with his pleasant smile.

But nobody met his eye and pace by pace, they closed in.

'Hey,' Trip said, turning on the spot while ensuring he remained in the centre of the circle. 'I know you're all annoyed about not getting paid, but I didn't steal your money.'

'But you know what happened to it,' Frank grunted.

'You got to believe me,' Trip said, holding his hands wide. 'I wouldn't steal from you. I'm a bartender, nothing more.'

'We ain't got time to argue,' Frank said. 'But we have got time to beat you to a pulp.'

Frank stormed in and hurled a huge round-armed blow at Trip's head. Trip ducked the blow and, deciding he couldn't talk his way out of this predicament, stood his ground and returned a flurry of blows to Frank's chest.

Frank took the blows, but just as Trip was drawing back a fist to punch his chin, a man paced in behind him and slapped firm hands on his shoulders, thrusting Trip to his knees.

And when he looked up, Frank delivered a backhanded swipe that wheeled him to the ground and a kick to the guts that lifted him off the dirt before rolling him into the feet of the circle of men.

Then the blows and kicks came strong and quick. Trip couldn't get in any retaliatory blows and he had to devote all his efforts to fighting his way back to his feet. And when he did, he saw that clear space had opened up before him.

He ran, but managed only two paces before someone swung a kick into the back of his knees and sent him tumbling. Then hands lifted him to his feet and held him firm. They swung him round to face Frank.

'You ready to talk while you still can?' Frank said, rolling his shoulders.

'I got nothing to say.'

Frank glared hard at him, but Trip looked beyond the group. Both sides of the river were deserted and the slope above was clear. He held out no hope that Grace would be able to free herself and rescue him.

He took deep breaths as he searched for a way to talk his way out of this predicament. No ideas came to him and, as he wasn't responding to Frank's taunts, Frank strode in. He gestured for the man holding Trip to release him then hammered a solid fist into his cheek that cracked his head to the side and sent him sprawling into the man who had been holding him. That man pushed him on to another, who in turn pushed him on to another, then another. Each man delivered short punches and digs, and they grew in strength as they goaded themselves on to administer a sustained beating.

Then one man delivered a blow that knocked Trip to the ground. On his knees he peered through the forest of legs around him and judged that he had only one hope. And it was a dangerous one – the river.

So he kept himself aware of where the river was as the next man dragged him to his feet and punched him on to the next man. That man also wheeled him away to the next, but with each blow he tumbled a few paces when he was facing the river and stood his ground when he wasn't. He rocked from one man to another, each time receiving jabs and blows, but each time getting nearer to the water.

When he was within ten yards of the water, one man hurled back his fist to hit him, but as that man had his back to the river, Trip threw himself forwards and grabbed him in a bear-hug.

Then he drove himself on, wheeling the man backwards until he slipped and the two men came crashing down, the boggy edge of the river splashing away around their bodies.

The man grunted and levered Trip off him. Trip didn't resist and let the man stand him straight, and when he pummelled his face, Trip staggered away into the shallows.

Only three men were standing up to their ankles in the water and Trip stomped to a halt then circled his opponent until that man stood between him and deeper water. Then he moved in. The man threw a punch at his head, but Trip ducked it. And when he came up, he hurled a huge pile-driving blow into the man's chin that cracked his head back and knocked his feet out of the water before he tumbled into the other men.

All three men went down, leaving clear space

between Trip and deeper water.

And this was the only opportunity Trip reckoned he'd get and he used his momentum to keep running. He vaulted the sprawling men then waded into the water until it was beyond his knees. At this point, the river bottom fell away sharply and he threw both hands up and dived in.

Biting cold hit him with solid force, as he threw out his arms trying to swim with strong strokes towards the surface. But when he broke the surface to gasp for air, the water swirled around him with too much strength for his wild strokes to be effective and the river took him downriver with Trip unable to control his movements.

He heard Frank shouting orders from the riverside and heard gun reports, but if they were well-aimed, he couldn't tell as the water was milling around him and masking any gunfire.

The angry force of the water dunked him, his open mouth gulping in cold water and, although he then closed his mouth, the water was grinding so much he couldn't tell if he was underwater or on the surface. He had to breathe or die and he thrust his arms and legs around, searching for buoyancy.

Long desperate moments passed without him gaining air, but then his thrashing about let his head break through the surface.

He glanced around, gulping air, and saw that he'd already headed around the first bend in the river and that Frank and the others were out of sight. Then the strong current dragged him under again and he had to fight to avoid it sucking him down permanently.

But his efforts were to no avail and through his blurred vision he saw the rocks on the river bottom. Then the huge shape of a boulder loomed ahead.

He fought to turn, getting his feet before him, and his boots hit the rock first, absorbing the impact. And he was even able to kick off from it and fight his way back to the surface.

But as he gulped in air, he saw what was ahead – boulders and more boulders, strewn across the river, the water a roiling mass of white atop muddy brown. But amidst the boulders was the towering expanse of the bridge, the main twin struts transfixed in the middle of the river and giving him hope that there would be something ahead he could grab hold of.

Then another boulder appeared in his path. He could do nothing but throw out his arms and he hit the boulder full in the chest. It blasted whatever air he had left in his body from him and he stood, treading water and transfixed, his arms and legs splayed.

He fought, searching for a handhold on the slippery rock, but the water rasped him away from the boulder. Buzzing filled his ears, the noise masking the roaring of the water, his vision dimming and not just from the grinding water. He needed to gather a full breath, but all he could claw into his tortured lungs was water.

Then a shape loomed ahead, large and solid. Trip fought his way to the surface to see that it was a bridge strut. This would be his last opportunity to avoid the river sweeping him on to his death, but he would miss it, perhaps by just five yards.

He frantically waved his arms and legs, the force of

the water not enabling him to deliver a full stroke. He didn't think he moved himself towards the strut, but he did fight himself above the water for long enough to gather a huge breath. And he saw that he had moved, perhaps a yard nearer the strut, but it was now just twenty yards downriver and he'd sweep by it in seconds.

He thrust out again with his legs, aiming to throw himself through the water, but a solid object battered into his back. Then it scraped against his cheek letting him confirm it was a broken bough, but although it pushed him underwater, he grabbed hold of the wood. And when he came up, he threw himself over it, caught hold of smaller branches, and hung on.

The bough slowed its journey downriver to swirl round in an eddy as it passed the strut, but he could do nothing but watch the strut drift by.

With a hopeless feeling descending on his water-bloated guts, he looked downriver and saw that he still had one more chance – ahead was the strut that supported the other side of the bridge, and between them a plank connected the struts. But Trip could only watch in hopeless and mounting horror as he floundered past his only possible way of escaping from the river.

He thrust out a hand over the bough, kicking with his feet, but the plank was out of reach and already he was closing on the final strut and his last chance. Then the bough shuddered.

Trip stretched his neck to see that the end of the bough had caught in the mass of detritus that was clinging hold of the bottom of the strut.

For a long moment, the bough held, keeping Trip stationary in the river with the powerful flow surging water over his body. Then the bough started to break free. The force swung Trip with it, winging him away from the plank between the struts. Trip had just seconds before the bough resumed its journey down-river and he dragged himself down the length of the bough, pushing himself through the water.

He clawed through the thick mass of broken branches that the strut had temporarily captured until, just as the bough tore free, Trip threw up an arm and his outstretched fingers grabbed a clawing hold of the plank. As the bough swirled away, he held on.

He trod water, catching his breath, then dragged himself out of the water and lay on his back, enjoying the simple pleasure of breathing. But then he started to shake from the cold and the shock and that forced him to turn his mind to more practical matters.

Within minutes, Frank and the others would return to the bridge and although they might presume he had drowned, he couldn't hide at the bottom of the gulch forever. And now was probably the only opportunity he'd get to leave without anyone seeing him.

So he scurried up the side of the gulch on hands and feet, hurrying to reach the top ahead of Frank. He leaned against each strut that dug into the side of the gulch and paused for breath before he moved on to the next strut, and quickly he reached the top.

His first sight on cresting the top was Grace. She

had been left alone and was now sitting by their horses with her head in her hands, and from the way she was shaking, Trip reckoned she was crying.

He glanced down the side of the river, confirming that Frank hadn't reached the top of the slope yet, then broke into a run.

'Grace,' he shouted, but the water clogging his lungs only let his word emerge as a coughing and spluttering noise.

But he shouted loud enough for Grace to hear him and she looked up, stared in shock at the dripping and staggering figure heading towards her, then jumped to her feet and hurried to him.

'You're alive,' she gasped, coming to a halt before him, her unfettered smile and watering eyes registering a mixture of joy and shock.

'Reckon as that's just about right,' Trip murmured. He staggered to a halt and coughed up water again. 'And at least you're pleased to see me.'

'Of course I am,' she gasped, placing a hand to her heart. 'They took my rifle and stopped me helping you. Then they . . . I thought they'd kill you.'

'Don't worry. I know you'd have helped if you could.'

'I would have,' she said. 'But if we don't get out of here soon, they will finish what they started.'

Trip glanced over his shoulder to the slope. Shouting was coming from beyond the edge of the slope. They had only seconds before Frank emerged and saw them.

CHAPTER 10

As the sounds of Frank calling to his men closed on the top of the slope, Trip and Grace ran to their horses. They mounted them and wasted no time in galloping away from the bridge.

They chose to head towards Calloway's Crossing and, as they reached a thin animal track that led through the trees and along which they'd have to ride single-file, Trip glanced back, seeing the first men clamber into view. Then the trees closed in behind him and cut off his view.

He sighed with relief but then, through the trees, a loud cry went up.

'She's gone,' someone shouted.

'And there's a trail of water over there. He got out the river.'

Trip shook the reins, but the action ripped pain through his chest and he bent to the side to spit up more water. Despite the urge to put distance between himself and the gulch, he reckoned he needed time to recuperate and between coughs, he gave Grace a pained look that said he was in no condition to escape from a determined pursuit.

Grace pointed to the side of the trail and Trip nodded. Then they jumped down from their horses and led them into the undergrowth. They were only twenty yards or so from the treeline and they could do nothing but keep still and hope their lack of movement would stop anyone noticing them.

In the clearing, Frank grouped his men together. Trip heard their comments and he was pleased to hear that nobody had picked up their trail from amongst the mass of everyone's hoofprints. And when they mounted up and thundered away from the bridge, they picked the route to Wagon Creek.

None of the workers stayed back and, with several sighs of relief, Trip and Grace looked at each other.

'You can relax,' Grace said. 'They won't get you now.'

'With your help they won't,' he said. 'But to be honest, I'm more pleased that you were worried about me. Perhaps it means you do care.'

'Don't say that, Trip Kincaid. Of course I care about you – as I would for any friend – and I hated thinking that my idea had got you killed.' She sighed and ventured a smile. 'So if it helps, I'll admit that helping Baxter was a bad idea.'

'Obliged you admitted that.'

'I'm a woman. I have no problem admitting I'm wrong.' She looked into the clearing. 'And now, as you're not fit enough to go anywhere fast, I need to do some thinking and work out what we should do next.'

Trip also considered the clearing around the

bridge. No ideas came to him, but when he turned back to look at Grace, a terrible and unpalatable thought came to him.

'The last few minutes have been rough for me,' he mused, 'and I don't want you getting all flustered, but I got a question and I'd be a fool not to ask it.'

Grace leaned forward, wincing. 'It isn't about last night, is it? Because I've told you, I'm not getting serious about you.'

'It is about last night, but not about that.' Trip took a deep breath. A voice in his head told him to keep this thought quiet, but he couldn't move on until he'd uttered it. 'I don't reckon you'd ... I reckon you wanted ...'

'Spit it out, Trip.'

Trip lowered his head and his voice. 'You'd shown no interest in me until that twenty thousand dollars was due to arrive, and then you distracted me and—'

'I distracted you!' Grace threw her hands high. 'You reckon I was working with Baxter and I *distracted* you while he planted the money on you?'

'Like I said,' Trip murmured, already regretting letting the dangers of the last few minutes force him into voicing such a wild theory. 'I don't want you getting all flustered. But I had to ask.'

'I'll get as flustered as I want, Trip Kincaid. And there was me getting all serious about you and then you go and say that.'

Trip cocked his head to one side. 'What's that about getting serious? You said you didn't want that.'

'Do you know nothing about women?'

Trip tipped back his hat. 'Seems as I don't know

nothing about this one.'

She swirled round to face the bridge and away from him.

'Then listen to this – I didn't side with Baxter. I didn't distract you.' She slapped her thigh and led her horse towards the clearing. 'And I sure as hell won't get serious about you now.'

Trip provided an apologetic smile to her receding back then hurried on to catch up with her, leading his horse, but as he closed on her, he saw that three riders were heading across the clearing toward them.

Grace flinched back and drew her horse to a halt before they could see them and Trip stopped beside her.

Then he recognized the lead rider as being the portly form of Marshal Kaplan and he glanced at Grace, who nodded. So they headed out from the trees and hailed him. Then, standing side by side, they awaited his arrival.

Trip searched for the right wording for his apology to Grace as he waited, but could think of nothing to say that wouldn't make things worse. And as the marshal rode closer, all thoughts of apologizing fled from his thoughts. The marshal was scowling and had already drawn his gun.

And his deputies didn't look happy either.

Trip narrowed his eyes as he watched the approaching Marshal Kaplan confer with his deputies, after which they spread out across the clearing before them.

'Kaplan,' Trip shouted. 'You heard what happened here?'

Kaplan didn't reply until he was twenty yards away.

'Sure have. Somebody stole twenty thousand dollars.'

'Got any leads?'

'Got one.' Kaplan gestured back at his deputies, who, as one, drew their guns and levelled them on Trip. 'You.'

Trip took the only action possible and raised his hands.

'I explained everything to Frank Moore. It wasn't me.'

'And when we get back to Wagon Creek, you can explain everything to me.' Kaplan pointed back down the trail. 'You can come quietly, or come face down over your horse. It's all the same to me.'

Trip flashed a glance at Grace, but she was already fluttering her eyelashes and leaning towards the marshal.

'Then I'll come quietly,' Trip said.

'And do you want me, Kappy?' Grace said.

'From what I've heard, you were with him last night, so you can come.' Kaplan smiled. 'But *you* don't need to be quiet.'

'I am so pleased,' she simpered. 'But I really don't want to go to Wagon Creek. I have business elsewhere.' She thrust out her chest to its utmost. 'And last night, I *was* with Trip, but the missing money didn't have anything to do with me. If you want, I can describe what we did, but you have a good memory, I'll let you work out the details for yourself.'

Kaplan slipped a finger into his collar and gulped.

'I guess I can do that. You can go.'

'Obliged,' Grace said, then mounted her horse and moseyed it past Kaplan, leaving slowly so that Kaplan and his deputies could linger their gazes on her.

As she left, she darted a glance over her shoulder at Trip, disguising the movement by flicking back her hair. But after their previous argument, Trip couldn't tell if her narrowed eyes meant she was leaving to help him, or was just leaving him to his fate.

'You don't need to put me in a cell while you check out my story,' Trip murmured.

'And you don't need to tell me how to do my job,' Kaplan said, peering at Trip through the bars.

'Then I'll tell you what happened. Someone stole the money. I didn't see who it was. I got nothing more than that.'

'But I ain't arrested you for what happened this morning. I've arrested you for what happened yesterday.' Kaplan raised his eyebrows. 'Ryan Trimble and four other men disappeared.'

Trip gritted his teeth. 'Don't know nothing about that.'

'And I don't suppose you know nothing about the note I received telling me to go to the woods a mile downriver from your saloon?'

'Who from?'

'That ain't important. What is important is what I found.' Kaplan folded his arms and waited for a response, but Trip remained silent. 'I found five bodies.'

'Ah,' Trip said.

116

A satisfied smile spread across Kaplan's podgy features before he headed to his desk. He sat, placed his feet on his desk, locked his hands behind his head, and shuffled round to face Trip.

'So I reckon you should tell me everything, starting from the moment you left me yesterday.'

Trip lowered his head while he collected his thoughts, then told the tale he'd rehearsed yesterday. When he'd finished, Marshal Kaplan fetched himself a mug of coffee.

'I'll recap,' he said. 'Your story is that Ryan Trimble demanded money off you. You tried to get Frank Moore to call him off, but he wasn't interested. You tried to get me interested, but failed. So you returned to Calloway's Crossing.'

'And this gunslinger was there.'

'And this gunslinger just happened to stop by, get into an argument with Ryan, then leave, but you reckon he might have ambushed and killed him later.'

'That's what I reckon.'

'And then you went to Calloway's Gulch for no good reason.'

'I went to make sure the workers had enjoyed themselves at my saloon and would come again.'

'My mistake. You went to ask that, but when you got there, you forgot to ask anyone if they'd enjoyed themselves.' Kaplan smiled. 'I checked. But you did decide to break in then spend the night in Adam Calloway's house, and while you and Grace were otherwise engaged the money arrived then was stolen, and you reckon this mysterious gunslinger took it.'

'I reckon.'

'And you know nothing about Adam Calloway's whereabouts?'

'No.'

'And you know nothing about the thousand dollars in your saddle-bag?'

'Nope.'

'And you reckon that story is more plausible than the simpler one that you killed Ryan and then stole the money?'

'It is, because it was this gunslinger.'

Kaplan took a long slurp of his coffee.

'And that would be this gunslinger that nobody has ever seen?'

'Not true. Grace saw him. And Chester and Isaac Wheeler did, too. They came to Wagon Creek. Ask them.'

'Good point.' Kaplan placed his mug on his desk then slapped his legs and stood. 'I will.'

'And when they agree with my story, you'll release me?'

Kaplan headed to the door, but stopped in the doorway.

'If they agree with your story, I'll arrest them and put them in the cell next to yours.'

'Why?'

'I may be an old lawman on the verge of retirement who's looking for a quiet life, but I know about the law and about people. When innocent people see a crime, no two ever see it the same. But when guilty people concoct a story, it's strange, but they always provide exactly the same story.'

'You can't lock us up because we support each other.'

'I can, but don't worry. A court won't convict you. Unless Chester is so weak-willed that when he's faced with jail, he changes his story.' Kaplan opened the door. 'You'd better hope he's too strong to do that.'

The lawman headed off, but returned within ten minutes. Whether he'd found Chester or Isaac and heard their stories, Trip didn't learn as he conferred with one of his deputies in low tones. Then he left again.

Trip paced back and forth, reckoning that if the marshal's plan was to make him sweat in the hope he'd tell the truth, it was a good one.

And as the morning wore on, Trip couldn't help but wonder what crimes Kaplan could deem him to have committed if he were to tell him everything. He had asked for Baxter's help in running Ryan out of Calloway's Crossing, but Baxter had done the killing. He had agreed to provide information to Baxter that'd help him steal twenty thousand dollars, and although Baxter had done that, he hadn't been involved in the raid.

Telling the truth might get him out of the trouble he was in, but might, if seen in an unfavourable light, drop him in even deeper trouble. And he was sure that Chester, and maybe Isaac, would put distance between themselves and the events of yesterday.

His brooding was becoming darker when Marshal Kaplan returned with Isaac Wheeler in tow. He didn't place in him in a cell, but let him sit at a spare desk while he wandered around his office, doing

119

nothing in particular.

As Isaac was sweating heavily while tugging at his clothes and shuffling on his seat, Trip tried to flash him an encouraging glance. But every time he looked his way, Marshal Kaplan happened to be looking at him, and Trip had to turn away.

Twenty minutes passed without Kaplan asking Isaac a single question. And by then, Isaac was dancing around on his seat as if he wanted to blurt out a full confession without Kaplan asking him anything.

Just as Kaplan was eyeing Isaac with anticipation and pacing purposefully towards him, Trip heard a horse pull up outside. He stood on his bunk to look through the cell window and his spirits lifted when he saw that Grace had arrived.

'And how can I help you?' Kaplan asked when Grace had come inside.

Grace nodded at Trip through the bars then smiled at the nervous Isaac, receiving a gulp in response.

'I've been asking around and I have information which proves Trip is innocent.' She paced towards Kaplan and placed a finger on his chest.

Kaplan looked at the finger and shrugged. 'And would that be real information or just pretty talk from a pretty woman?'

'And you are such a tease.' She smiled, but then removed the smile. 'But this time, it's real.'

'It'd better be good, because I'll need plenty to release Trip.'

'It is good. And it's just a name.' Grace leaned forwards and whispered in Kaplan's ear.

Kaplan paled and flinched back. 'You sure?'

'Never more so.'

'But . . .' Kaplan looked to the ceiling, sighing, then called for the keys. Without further word, he glanced at Isaac then pointed at the door.

Isaac didn't need any encouragement to hurtle outside, slamming the door shut behind him, as Kaplan unlocked the cell door and gestured for Trip to leave, too.

'Obliged,' Trip said, as he joined Grace. 'But what did you say to prove my story?'

'Just the name of the man who's behind everything that's been happening to us for the last few days.' Grace sighed and exchanged an irritated glance with Marshal Kaplan. 'And that name is Milton Calloway.'

CHAPTER 11

Trip didn't dare to ask any questions while they were in the marshal's office. He was just pleased the marshal had released him.

Marshal Kaplan did follow him out, but only to report he wouldn't waste his time investigating another one of Milton Calloway's schemes, then returned to his office.

'What you got to say?' Grace asked when they reached their horses.

'Thanks.'

'Anything else?'

Trip considered. 'Well, as you seem to know more about this situation than I do, I guess I'd like to know what's happening.'

'Calloway's double-crossing again,' she reported, her eyes showing her irritation and her jaw tensing with a suggestion that she'd expected him to say something else. 'There isn't nothing more to it than that.'

Trip nodded, noticing Isaac loitering further down the boardwalk. He beckoned him and the young man shuffled closer.

'Trip,' Isaac said, his shoulders hunched and his hands shaking. 'I wouldn't have talked no matter what Kaplan did to me.'

'Of course you wouldn't,' Trip said, trying to sound convincing.

Isaac sighed with relief and looked up, his shaking stopping.

'You going off to get Milton now?'

'Yeah.'

Isaac stood tall. 'Then take me with you. I wasn't nervous in there for what I might reveal. It was because I ain't happy about Pa making me run out on you.'

'I can understand that. But relax. You and I don't have a problem.'

'That mean I can come anyhow?'

Trip nodded then mounted his horse and, with a subdued whoop, Isaac hurried away to collect his horse.

At a steady pace, Trip, Grace and Isaac headed out of town then swung round on to the trail to Calloway's Crossing.

'Why are you so sure Baxter didn't steal the money and that Milton's behind this?' Trip asked.

'And why are you avoiding the subject?' she said, her eyes narrowing as she swirled round in the saddle.

'What subject?'

'If you don't know . . .' Grace sighed. 'As you only care about Milton, I'll tell you this – Milton Calloway is the biggest double-crossing snake that's ever lived around these parts, and what's been happening to us is precisely the sort of thing he'd organize.'

Trip shrugged. 'I believe that double-crosser is capable of doing anything, but when I left him he was heading away from here. He's got no reason to return.'

'Other than to steal his brother's fortune.'

'You'll need more than that.'

'Adam Calloway's disappeared.'

Despite Trip's contempt for Milton and his growing belief that she could be right, he shrugged.

'Could be plenty of reasons for that.'

'There could, but I did myself some thinking and none of this feels right. Three weeks ago you stopped Ryan Trimble killing Milton and in gratitude Milton gave you Calloway's Crossing, but then by a huge coincidence, Ryan arrives and demands money off you. And he's also the man who should have been guarding the money that was destined for Adam Calloway.'

Trip felt blocks of thought rearrange themselves in his mind. And he didn't like their new shape.

'I knocked myself out when I tried to save Milton,' he said, speaking slowly. 'Ryan had been all set to kill Milton, but when I came to, he'd gone. I guess Milton could have bargained for his life by telling Ryan about his brother's money. And Ryan could have come here to protect the money when he was really planning to steal it. And the plan would have worked if Baxter hadn't have happened by.'

'But it did work.' Grace glanced at Isaac.

'You don't know Milton as well as we do,' Isaac

said. 'His schemes are devious. Even Baxter killing Ryan could have been part of it.'

'You mean Milton hired Baxter?' Trip asked.

'Perhaps,' Grace said, 'or maybe he used the distraction he provided to steal the money for himself.'

'Or maybe both,' Isaac said.

Trip continued to question them as he tried to piece together how Milton could have manufactured his recent predicament. Adam Calloway's comment echoed in his mind that when dealing with Milton, free was often the highest price any man could pay, but even so, he couldn't see how Milton could be behind everything.

But Isaac and Grace were convinced that Milton was behind this, and it was only when they were a mile from the river and Grace reported they were being followed that Trip accepted what had happened.

He glanced back, narrowing his eyes, and although the rider was around a mile away, he reckoned it had to be Baxter.

And with that sight, the final piece of Milton's plan fitted into place in his mind. And so did the way he'd defeat him.

'We're stopping in Calloway's Crossing,' he announced.

'But Baxter's following us,' Grace said. 'We have to run.'

'We don't. You no longer have to be the one who does all the thinking. I'm thinking now, and I've decided to start thinking like Milton.'

Grace and Isaac looked at each other then nodded in support, but Trip wasn't as confident as he sounded and he took the precaution of speeding up as they closed on the river. The others hurried to join him and at a fair trot they rode into the deserted Calloway's Crossing. Behind them, Baxter was gaining fast, but they still had several minutes before he arrived.

Trip reckoned he had enough time, provided his assumptions were correct. And he discovered the first was right when they headed into the saloon and found Adam Calloway lying tied up and gagged behind the bar. Adam was dirt-streaked and when Isaac sawed a knife through the bonds tying his hands behind his back, he needed all three of them to lever him to his feet.

While Isaac searched for a jug of beer, Trip drew Grace aside and whispered quick instructions to her, his brisk tone not inviting any discussion. She nodded and hurried outside, not needing to wait until he completed his explanation. Then he checked on Adam.

'Milton?' he asked.

'None other,' Adam croaked, then swung away to dry spit to the side.

Isaac arrived with a jug and Adam snatched it from his grasp. He poured the beer down his throat, most of it cascading onto his chest, but he gulped and gulped before finally withdrawing the jug and beaming as if that had been the finest drink he'd ever consumed.

'Where is he?' Trip asked.

'He can't have gone far.' Adam nodded towards the door. 'He heard you coming and ran.'

Adam's comment reminded Trip of the urgency of the situation and one look at the haggard and bone-weary Adam and the eager but youthful Isaac convinced him he'd have to deal with Baxter on his own.

'You two,' he said. 'Stay in here and keep your heads down, no matter what Baxter does.'

'But you ain't got no gun,' Isaac said.

'A gun wouldn't help me. To defeat a fast-draw gunslinger like Baxter, I need to out-think him.'

Trip didn't wait for any more comments and hurried outside.

Baxter was still a minute away from Calloway's Crossing, his horse thundering up dust in his wake, giving Trip enough time to discover whether his decision to think like Milton would work. He hurried along the side of the saloon to the top of the bank then paced down into the dry gully.

Milton Calloway had been behind everything that had happened recently. He'd told Ryan how he could steal his brother's money. He'd hired Baxter to double-cross Ryan. He'd witnessed Ryan's shooting, seen where they'd taken the bodies, and left a note for Marshal Kaplan implicating Trip. And he'd stolen the money from Calloway's Gulch then planted some of it on Trip. But Adam was the only person who had seen him and that meant he had a good hiding place, and one that was close to Calloway's Crossing.

And Trip reckoned he knew where it was.

Ever since he'd built the saloon, he'd wondered

about the growing heap of dirt that a burrowing animal had made in the bank, but now that he'd entertained his suspicions, the heap didn't look as if it'd been pawed away.

The animal that had made the heap was larger and was more used to double-crossing than burrowing.

Trip hunkered down on the mound, fingering the dirt and running his gaze over the fresh earth. And now that he knew what to look for, he saw the outline of a length of wood and perhaps matting buried beneath the dirt.

'Now,' he said. 'I wonder what's down here. I'm mighty worried this animal could be dangerous. I reckon as I might stick dynamite down this here hole and get rid of it.'

Trip brushed away dirt while he waited, not that he expected an immediate answer, freeing what did prove to be cloth.

'I said,' he uttered, kneeling down and fingering the cloth. 'I got dynamite and I'm going to stick it down this here hole.'

He shook the cloth, freeing a wider stretch and confirming that it covered a hole and then a tunnel that led beneath the saloon.

'Now I just hope no person is down here or they ain't going to like it when they get blown to pieces.'

'All right,' a voice murmured from under the ground. 'Don't do it.'

'Milton Calloway,' Trip snapped. 'You double-crossing toad.'

A corner of the cloth raised and a face peered out

– Milton Calloway's.

'How you figure out I was here?' he asked, blinking rapidly at the brightness as he clutched a bulging bag to his chest.

'I started thinking like you. And now you're coming out with the money, and we can put an end to this.'

Milton moved to slip back into his hole, but Trip grabbed his collar and dragged him out on to the bank.

Milton squirmed, but Trip kicked him towards the top of the bank, and with Milton before him they reached ground level as Baxter rode into Calloway's Crossing.

In short order, Baxter dismounted and one steady pace at a time headed towards them, both guns drawn with one aimed towards the saloon and the other at Trip. He stopped ten feet away, his jaw having the same firmness as it'd had when he'd blasted Ryan Trimble away.

'You should have run, Trip,' he said. 'Now, you die.'

'I won't,' Trip said. 'I've been double-crossed, too. But I've put an end to that. Give him the bag, Milton.'

Milton looked at the bag then at Baxter.

'I guess . . .' Milton gulped, his hands shaking, and the bag slipped from his grasp to land at his feet.

Baxter watched the bulging bag topple over on its side then raised his eyebrows.

'The money?'

'It sure is,' Trip said.

'Then come closer,' Baxter urged. Neither Trip nor Milton moved, so he ripped off a shot that thudded into the bag before emerging and whistling past Milton's leg.

Milton danced back a pace then, as if he'd finally accepted he wouldn't get away with the money now, lowered his head. Then he did a double-take and ran, his arms wheeling as he kicked up his heels and hurtled over the edge of the bank.

Trip craned his neck to follow Milton's progress, watching him hightail it down the dry gully, heading for the river.

Within a minute, he reached the boggy extremity of the river. Only then did he emerge from the gully, but he hurried off downriver towards Calloway's Gulch. And he didn't look back.

Baxter snorted. 'That leaves you to give me the money, then.'

Trip nodded then picked up the bag. Inside he could hear the bills rustling as they shifted position. He opened the flaps to glance inside, seeing the wads of bills that could well come to nineteen thousand dollars, then swung them closed and faced Baxter.

He swung the bag back and forth, appearing as if he was about to throw it to Baxter's feet, but at the full extent of his backwards swing, he released the bag. It flew end over end, heading beyond the bank, and disappeared from view.

'Why?' Baxter muttered, pacing to the side to peer down into the gully.

The bag came to a rolling halt on the gully bottom and, on the last roll, the flaps swung open and spilled wads of bills over the dirt.

'You want the money,' Trip said, folding his arms. 'You get it.'

Baxter narrowed his eyes. 'What you planning?'

'Nothing.'

With a nudge of his wrist, Baxter gestured to the bottom of the gully.

'Then fetch it.'

'I won't.'

Baxter loosed off a shot, the slug tearing into the dirt at Trip's feet.

'The next one will be four feet higher.'

Trip glanced down at the furrow the bullet had torn out of the earth then shrugged and headed down into the gully. Baxter followed him to stop on the top of the bank.

Trip didn't hurry. He paced down to the bag, righted it, then placed the spilt wads into it one at a time, but a slug tore through the top of the bag.

'Hurry,' Baxter urged. 'Last warning.'

With still more than half of the wads spilled out beside the bag, Trip stood.

'I am hurrying.' He smiled. 'But you'd better take the money now or it'll be heading to Calloway's Gulch.'

'What you—?' Baxter flinched as a huge explosion ripped out nearby.

Trip glanced over his shoulder to see that Grace had lit the fuse at just the right time. Rocks from Chester's dam hurtled into the air as if they were thrown pebbles, a huge cloud of dust blossoming out from a blast that had ripped the top of the hill away.

Then the dammed creek surged out from beneath

the dust, a trickle at first, but growing to become a solid wave hurtling down the gully.

'Here comes the water,' Trip shouted. 'And it'll take the money with it. What you going to do?'

Baxter swirled round to confront Trip, his gun arcing down to aim at him. Trip returned his gaze, but saw nothing in Baxter's cold eyes to suggest he wouldn't shoot. He dropped to his knees and hurled the wads into the bag.

He glanced up as he shovelled, seeing the water surging towards him, closing at a relentless pace and now under one hundred yards away.

'Hurry!' Baxter shouted from the top of the bank and even edging a few paces down the bank towards him.

'I'm going as fast as I can.' Trip broke off with several wads still on the ground. 'Unless you want me to leave it for the water to take.'

'Quit wasting time.'

Trip glanced up to see the first surge of water was fifty yards away, a towering wall of water another ten yards back.

With Baxter urging him on, he stayed on his knees until every last bill was in the bag, but by then the first trickle of water was lapping at his feet. He yanked the bag up, loose bills spilling away to land in the water, then ran for the bank, but already the wall of water was closing on him.

He thrust his head down and ran, but he slipped in the shallow water and went to his knees and when he came up, the huge surge of water was looming over him.

'Throw me the bag,' Baxter shouted.

Trip yanked back his arm and launched the bag towards Baxter, but his weak throw let it land halfway up the bank and ten feet before him. Baxter glanced at the approaching water, seeing that it'd sweep Trip away then the bag within seconds, then rushed down the bank.

His hand closed on the bag handle and he tugged it up, but then grunted as a length of the bank fell away beneath his feet. He tumbled straight down, the deep hole that Milton had dug there and covered with matting then dirt giving way to plummet him downwards.

It would take Baxter only seconds to fight his way out, but Trip reckoned the water would do the main damage. As Baxter vented his anger by firing high, Trip hurtled up the bank, the water tearing at his heels, and threw himself over the top of the bank to lie flat.

He swirled round on his belly to watch the water surge by, some falling away to pile into the hole. Baxter's hand clawed up over the edge of the hole and dug into the ground, but then the force of the water yanked that hand away and a moment later the water filled the hole with muddy, swirling water.

Amidst the water, he saw Baxter's body bob to the surface, but by then, he was another thirty yards down the creek.

And when Adam and Isaac emerged from the saloon to join him in standing on the top of the bank, they all watched the creek return to its former placid self.

But by now, Adam Calloway's fortune and Baxter had been swept away into the main river.

CHAPTER 12

Trip slapped Adam's back as he offered his commiserations about the loss of the money.

'I'd hoped I could entice Baxter into falling into the hole without losing the money,' he said. 'I'm sorry I failed.'

Adam shrugged. 'I should have known it'd come to this when I ran Milton out of town instead of shooting him.'

'You could never do that to your own brother.'

Adam snorted. 'Try losing eighteen thousand dollars because of that useless varmint, then say that.'

Trip had one small piece of good news and he decided to wait until Grace returned before revealing it. But unlike the previous time Trip had survived a seemingly inevitable death, when she hurried back into the crossing, she didn't appear pleased to see him.

She flounced to a halt before the saloon and stood with one leg thrust out and her arms folded, her angry eyes driving all thought of the good news from Trip's mind.

'Well?' she demanded.

'I'm obliged for your help,' he said. 'Again.'

'And?'

'And what?'

'Trip Kincaid, you're either the most stupid man I've ever met, or the most stupid man in the world. Which is it?'

'I don't know what you mean.'

Grace looked skywards. 'What did you say before Marshal Kaplan arrested you?'

Trip tracked back over the events of the last few hours until he remembered they had argued after he'd said something he shouldn't have.

'Ah.' He shrugged. 'But I've been arrested, released, nearly got shot by a gunslinger, and nearly got drowned. Surely my stupid comment about you *distracting* me ain't that important after all that.'

'It might not be important to you, but if I'm ever going to get serious about you again, it is to me.'

Trip took a deep breath. 'In that case, I need to say sorry for what I said.'

She paced to him and slapped his right arm then narrowed her eyes and slapped his other arm.

'I can't believe you thought I'd helped to steal the money.'

'I just did me some thinking and the way I saw it, if you didn't want me, that meant you wanted something else.'

'And the only thing you could think of was the money?'

'Yeah.'

'And now you know you're wrong, why do you

think I said I didn't want you?'

Trip considered. He had a horrible feeling that anything he said would come out wrong or she'd twist his words, but he decided to venture his most honest opinion.

'I guess the reason is simple. You wanted a way out of being a saloon-girl and if you were nice to me, we might run a saloon in Wagon Creek together. But I guess you were worried that—'

'Trip Kincaid,' she screeched.

Trip's guts rumbled, now wishing he'd stuck with his original idea of apologizing for everything he'd ever said and ever done and hoping she'd forgive him.

'I guess that's wrong, too.'

She stamped a foot. 'It sure is. I can't believe you. You apologize for saying one bad thing and then say something even worse. Why can't you just understand me? I didn't want a way out of my troubles because I haven't got any. I just wanted you.'

'You just wanted me?' Trip intoned slowly.

'Yeah. I *did* want you, but I don't want you now. I wouldn't come back to you even if you begged me.' She shook her head. 'And to think of what I did for you.'

'You did nothing. You said you didn't want to get serious.'

'Don't tell me what I said, Trip Kincaid.'

Trip took a deep breath, searching for the right thing to say, but unable to work out what that might be.

'Then don't get serious. We were a good team and

we can just look after a saloon together.' Trip risked a smile. 'And if we ever feel like getting friendly again one day, we can—'

'I will never feel like getting friendly with you ever again. This saloon can fall down for all I care.'

She swirled round and kicked the corner of the building, and although she hit it with some strength, Trip was surprised to see the walls wobble and hear a dangerous creak issue from the wood.

Grace danced out of the way, but the corner of the saloon had now veered at an angle, and inch by inexorable inch it was doing what she'd hoped it'd do and falling over.

Trip glanced at the creek running by and winced.

He'd built the saloon on the side of the dry gully and that was now the side of the creek. But the first flush of water running down it in a month would have washed into the tunnel Milton had dug.

And that tunnel led beneath the saloon.

Everyone hurried out of the way as, with much creaking and cracking, the third saloon at Calloway's Crossing collapsed in upon itself, leaving just a heap of broken wood. And as the dust settled, that gently subsided into a new stretch of mud.

'Well,' Trip said. 'I guess there ain't nothing more for us here now.'

'There isn't,' Grace said, standing before him, her eyes now cold and distant. 'When you rode into town, I was just a saloon-girl in Wagon Creek, and that's what I can be again.'

With a determined stamp of her foot, she headed to her horse. Trip couldn't help but watch her walk away, but the firm set of her back and the blankness of his mind as to what he could say forced him to accept he couldn't stop her leaving.

He turned to look at his saloon. It was beyond repair, but he tried to console himself with the thought that now the creek had changed to its original direction, his land would stop being so muddy.

But no matter how he looked at it, running a saloon without Grace wasn't an appealing thought and he might have ridden out of town if Adam hadn't have pointed downriver towards the gulch.

'I can't stay to help you here,' he said. 'I have to get Milton.'

'You do that,' Trip said, 'but you'll have to do it on your own. I've wasted enough time on your family dispute. I'm leaving.'

'Only if you can. Milton set you and Grace up to take the blame, and just because he didn't get the money, it won't stop him telling everyone a very different story than what's just happened.'

Trip glanced at Grace, who had now mounted up, but she had turned at the mention of her name and was nodding.

'And I guess,' she said, 'there's only one place he'll go to tell that story.'

'Yeah,' Adam said. 'Calloway's Gulch.'

Trip nodded. He told Isaac to see if he could salvage anything from the saloon then hurried to his horse. As Adam mounted up, she glared at Trip, who provided a shrug.

'I said some things I didn't mean to,' he said, venturing a smile. 'But that's only because I—'

'But that's only because you're an idiot, Trip Kincaid, and I was an idiot to waste my time getting all serious out you. So remember this – just because I'm coming with you, it doesn't mean I want to spend time with you.'

Trip limited himself to a nod and in a line they headed down the creek. When they reached the side of the river, they waded through the creek then picked up Milton's footprints, but they ended a hundred yards into the trees at a small campsite.

Clearly, Milton hadn't hidden in the hole beneath the saloon all the time and Trip also saw that he'd left a horse here to collect.

So they galloped downriver to the gulch, the tired and sore Adam bringing up the rear, and when they reached the clearing around the bridge, Trip was glad they'd hurried. Milton had arrived first and was already blurting out an explanation of the events of the last few days to Frank Moore. And from Frank's thunderous expression, most of Milton's version blamed Trip and Grace.

'Those people stole then destroyed the money,' Milton shouted, pointing a firm finger at them.

All the workers who had previously tried to kill Trip had returned and they were an eager audience to this tale. As one, they swung round to face Trip with Frank at the front.

'And that includes our wages,' Frank said, advancing on Trip. 'You got a lot of explaining to do.'

With Grace at his side and Adam behind, Trip dismounted and stood before the arc of disgruntled bridge workers.

'You got one thousand dollars of your wages,' Trip said, standing his ground, 'and Adam's accepted he won't see his cut of the money again.'

Adam grunted his support for Trip, his comments forcing Frank into temporary silence and when he spoke again, his voice wasn't so belligerent.

'That's as maybe, but it still leaves us short by a thousand.'

'Yeah,' Milton shouted from behind Frank. 'You all worked for nothing because of Trip.'

Frank grunted his agreement then gestured to the men around him, who all took a long pace towards Trip.

'And so,' Frank said, cracking his knuckles, 'there ain't nothing you can say that'll get you out of that beating that's been coming to you.'

Trip waited until Frank was two paces away then opened his jacket.

'Then it's a good job I managed to reclaim some of the money. I just had time to stuff a couple of handfuls into my pocket.'

Trip removed a huge wad of bills from his pocket and waved it, the flash of green stopping everybody in their tracks. Frank's eyes gleamed as Trip counted out the money he'd saved into his other hand. It came to nearly fifteen hundred dollars and Trip didn't need to mention it was enough to pay the wages and still leave a few hundred dollars for Adam.

And when Trip held the money out to Frank, the foreman smiled.

'Obliged,' he said. 'Perhaps I got you wrong, Trip.'

'You can't believe him,' Milton shouted from

behind the group.

'I can,' Frank said. 'My men will get paid and if your brother ain't concerned about not getting his money, the matter is closed.'

Milton darted his gaze around, looking for support, but the workers were now ignoring him and pestering Frank to be paid.

Trip guessed what Milton's next action would be and he slipped round Frank to block the route to Milton's horse, but Milton turned on his heel and ran to the bridge instead. Trip looked at Adam, but he'd sat down to massage his tired limbs and he looked up and provided a resigned shake of the head that said he wouldn't waste his limited energy chasing after Milton. But Grace was rubbing her hands and taking deep breaths.

'I've kept my temper for far too long,' she said, heading to the bridge. 'You just aren't worth shouting at, Trip Kincaid, but I reckon Milton can do with some suffering.'

Grace maintained her steady pacing, her deliberate steps showing that Milton would be on the receiving end of an anger that had been growing since Trip had annoyed her. Milton reached the bridge first, looked back at Grace, then took his first tentative steps onto the structure.

Trip followed to see how this situation would unfold and he quickly saw that Milton had made a big mistake. He didn't have Grace's head for heights and after only a few steps along the bridge framework, he was already holding his arms wide and swaying, while she paced on to the bridge, her stride and demeanour unconcerned.

'You sure you want to head across the gulch?' she asked. 'I thought you were scared of heights.'

'I am,' Milton murmured. He took another pace, but his legs shook and he had to stand sideways and wheel his arms to avoid falling. 'Go away.'

Grace took several long paces to catch up with him then pushed him along the framework.

'Not doing that. After everything I did for you, you nearly got me killed.'

Milton risked several running paces until his foot slipped and he went to his knees. He grabbed hold of both sides of the plank and wrapped his arms around it, hugging the plank as if it would save his life. From the side of the gulch, Trip thought he heard him whimper.

'I didn't mean to,' Milton pleaded. 'I only tried to get Trip.'

'But I cared for Trip and you took that away.' She took another confident step to stand over Milton. 'Don't look down. You might fall.'

Milton edged his head to the side to look down, gulped, then fell to his chest and pressed his cheek to the comforting plank, but Grace jumped up and down behind him, shaking the plank. Milton swayed from side to side then crawled away from her one tentative, shuffled pace at a time, but he wasn't even halfway across the gulch yet and Trip reckoned Grace would make him suffer over every tortured pace.

Trip edged onto the end of the plank and folded his arms. He knew that Grace's anger was really directed at him and he didn't like to ponder why she was taking it out on Milton instead, but either way, he relished watching Milton get his comeuppance. He glanced down at the swirling water, wondering if Grace would make Milton fall to his death, but then darted his gaze to the side when he saw a black object bob up in the water.

He gulped, noting that they were downriver from Calloway's Crossing and, as they'd come here quickly, Baxter's body would pass by them if it hadn't snagged on something en route. He narrowed his eyes as he watched the object swirl closer, but then saw that it wasn't a body.

It was the bag containing Adam's money and it'd reach the bridge in less than a minute.

Grace was standing over the crying and pleading Milton and loudly venting her anger at him and the bridge workers were all congregating around Frank several hundred yards away. Trip judged he'd waste too much time getting anyone's attention. So he jumped off the plank and made his way down the side of the gulch.

Many branches from spindly trees and bushes were on the side of the gulch and Trip broke one off to hook the passing bag. The bank was slippery and he had to rock back on his heels to avoid sliding down the gulch.

But he reached the bottom ahead of the bag and shuffled along the bottom plank to gain a good position. He knelt down on the same spot where a few hours earlier he had dragged himself from the river then poked the branch out into the water and waited for the bag to swirl closer.

He would have only one opportunity to hook it, but when he lunged, the branch slid through the handle. He offered a silent prayer of thanks for his good fortune then raised the bag high above the water and slopped it down on the plank beside him.

He sat, taking deep breaths with his feet dangling over the edge, then opened the bag.

The money inside was sodden and he guessed that some of it would be missing, but enough of it should remain to please Adam.

Trip looked up. Above him, he could see Milton's arms and legs wrapped around a plank and see Grace's foreshortened profile, both people oblivious to Trip's discovery as Grace shouted taunts. Trip smiled as he stood, but then something snagged his foot and dragged him back down to his knees.

He glanced over the side. A hand had emerged from the river and was clutching his ankle. Then the soaked Baxter swung into view, hanging on beneath the plank, his time in the water having failed to dampen the bloodlust that burned in his eyes.

He walked his hand up Trip's leg to gather a firmer grip, then tugged.

CHAPTER 13

Trip rolled back, tearing his leg from Baxter's grasp and, while still kneeling, pushed himself back along the plank.

Baxter emerged from the water, dripping wet and vengeful, but Trip did notice that he'd lost his gun, perhaps discarding it to reduce weight.

Trip waited for long enough to grab the bag then rolled to his feet and ran for the slope. Baxter dashed after him and the two men hurried up the slope with Baxter's stomping footfalls pounding behind Trip and closing. And after only thirty yards of climbing, Baxter lunged and grabbed for Trip, getting a hold of his chest.

The two men went down, but Trip twisted, landing on his back, then kicked out, knocking Baxter away. Then he rolled onto the plank beneath the top of the bridge. He gained his footing then turned and kicked out, aiming for Baxter's head and trying to tumble him back down the slope, but the light-footed Baxter swerved away from the kick then vaulted on to the plank. He spread his hands wide, blocking Trip's route to the top of the gulch and, with no choice, Trip backed away along the plank.

Milton and Grace were twenty feet above him on the top of the bridge. The noise had alerted Grace and she was peering over the side to watch them.

'Is that the money?' she shouted.

'Yeah,' Trip murmured, backing away. 'But don't celebrate just yet.'

Trip backed another pace, but then made a sudden decision. Grace was as sure-footed as Baxter was and he guessed she'd be equally sure-handed. He shouted up a warning then launched the bag in the air. He kept his gaze on Baxter and aside from watching the bag's shadow rise up the side of the gulch from the corner of his eye, the only confirmation that Grace had caught it was Baxter's grunt.

Trip considered jumping down, but even though he'd backed only ten paces along the plank, the ground below had fallen away sharply and there was already a considerable drop of twenty or more feet. And before him, Baxter was pacing along the plank, and like Grace, he strode with assurance and no suggestion that the height concerned him.

Trip glanced over his shoulder and saw that the plank carried on until it reached the strut in the river. Then a second plank provided an abrupt right turn running downriver to the next strut. Another plank then headed back to the side of the gulch.

With his route decided, Trip turned, swayed until he stood firmly, then paced along the plank as quickly as he dared. Behind him, he heard Baxter stomping closer with assurance in his stride, but Trip reached the central strut with no problem then swung a foot around the strut to reach the next plank.

Baxter's footfalls pattered behind him and with Trip off-balance, Baxter lunged and grabbed his collar from behind, then tugged backwards.

Trip wheeled his arms frantically before wrapping them around the strut. His outstretched foot searched for the next plank but landed on air and he hung on with Baxter holding him away from the strut and gradually applying more pressure.

'The money, now,' he grunted.

'I gave it to Grace.'

'And she'll give it to me, or I'll pull you down.' Baxter glanced down at the swirling water, over one hundred feet below. 'And you'll drown, provided the fall doesn't kill you.'

Trip made the mistake of looking down at the milling water, the action making his head spin, then dragged his gaze upwards. He couldn't see either Grace or Milton, but from a shadow over the side of the bridge, he decided that Grace was standing above them.

'I guess I don't want that.'

'Then give the order.'

Baxter released his grip slightly to encourage Trip, but Trip used that mistake to swing around the strut. His foot landed on the next plank and with the leverage that gave him, he dragged himself clear of Baxter's grip, the effort throwing him to his knees and his momentum sprawling him over the side.

He had a gut-churning moment when he was staring down at the water below. Then he dragged himself up to lie on his back, staring up. And it was to face Baxter who had swung around the strut and was looming over him.

Trip pushed himself back a foot, but not too far. He doubted he could gain his feet and run before Baxter grabbed him, but lying like this, Baxter could get too close and he might be able to kick his legs from under him.

But Baxter must have been aware of the danger and he stayed back.

'No more tricks,' he said. 'The money, now, or I shoot you.'

'You lost your gun in the river.'

Baxter shrugged, the action drawing a pistol from his sleeve.

'I lost *one* gun.'

Trip looked up, searching for Grace, but couldn't locate her shadow at first. Then he saw it. And it was above him and several feet away from Baxter. And he also saw the tightly wrapped rope around the plank.

Trip suppressed a gulp as he deduced Grace's reckless plan then turned back to face Baxter.

'All right,' he said, then shuffled backwards along the plank.

'Then stop backing away and do it.'

Trip did as ordered and sat up. He spread his hands, shrugging, and his seeming acquiescence encouraged Baxter to advance a short pace. Trip risked a glance up to confirm he was directly below the coil of rope then nodded.

'Grace,' he shouted. 'Give it to him, now!'

A momentary smile twitched the corners of Baxter's mouth, but then died as a shadow swooped over him.

He glanced to the side, but it was to see Grace leaping from the bridge above, a short plank in her hands and a rope around her waist. She swung in a short arc, the plank thrust back to its utmost and, as she reached Baxter, she swung it round, aiming for Baxter's head.

With lightning reactions, Baxter ducked, the plank and Grace whirling over his head, but as Grace swung off on an arc over the river, Trip kicked out, his boot crunching into Baxter's ankle.

Baxter's foot slipped and he fell to one knee. Trip kicked again, connecting with the knee and this time, Baxter rocked backwards. Trip threw his hands back, raised his body from the plank, and kicked out with all his might, but Baxter jerked back and the wild kick missed, throwing Trip over the side of the plank.

Without any control of his movement, he slipped downwards until more than half his body was over the side. He clung on with his wet hands splayed and gripping the wood, but then his hands slipped and he fell.

In desperation, he lunged. His grasp closed around Baxter's calf and he hung on with his body dangling and his legs wheeling.

Baxter braced himself, his pistol arcing round to aim down at him, but behind Baxter, Grace had reached the extent of her upwards swing and was returning for a second pass.

Baxter saw Trip's gaze dart to her swooping form and he swirled round to confront her, but with Trip holding his leg he couldn't turn fully and even when he ducked, Grace had anticipated the action. She swung the plank downwards, slamming it into Baxter's midriff and, with her momentum behind the blow, pushed him over the side.

Trip reckoned that was a good moment to release his grip of Baxter's leg and he hurled a hand forward to grip the plank as Baxter tumbled by. A few seconds later, he heard a crash as Baxter hit another plank on the way down followed by a splash.

Trip floundered with just one hand holding him up then hurled his free hand to the plank. He hung on and ventured a glance down to see Baxter's body swirl away downriver with his face down, but in his precarious position that just made him giddy.

He tore his gaze away and fought to climb back on to the plank, but he couldn't summon the strength. With nothing for his feet to touch to gain purchase, the best he could do was to secure his position with his arms locked and his body relaxed and straight.

He looked up and watched Grace swing gently back and forth. She was tearing at her rope, but with it supporting her weight, she wasn't having any effect.

'We need help,' Trip shouted.

'I know that, Trip Kincaid,' Grace shouted back, then pointed up. 'And Milton's the closest.'

Trip and Grace exchanged a long wince.

'And I suppose you left the money up there with him.'

'I did.' Grace sighed. 'And that's the last mistake I'll ever make with that no-good, good-for—'

'Hey,' a voice shouted from above. 'I heard that.'

A rope dropped down, gradually unfurling to dangle beside Trip, who looked up to see Milton peer over the edge before gulping then darting back. Then Milton shuffled into view, still crawling and shaking with each pace.

'You stayed,' Trip said, unable to keep the surprise from his tone.

'I may be many things,' Milton said. 'But I'd never desert a woman when she's dangling over the side of a bridge.'

Grace nodded. 'I guess even you must have principles – just.'

'I *do* have principles,' Milton said, his tone hurt as he held his head high. Then he looked along the bridge and shrugged. 'And Frank and about ten other men have got guns on me.'

CHAPTER 14

Ten minutes after disposing of Baxter, Trip and Grace were safely back on solid ground. They sat on the edge of the gulch while Frank sent men off to search downriver for Baxter, but Trip reckoned they'd only find a body.

Milton hunkered down as he watched Adam kneel beside the bag and fish the sodden money from it.

'Take your eyes off that,' Grace said, 'or I'll. . . .'

Milton glanced down into the gulch and gulped.

'That mean you're still going to throw me off the bridge?'

'I sure will.' Grace considered the growing heap of money then sighed and waved at him in a dismissive manner. She softened her voice. 'I wasn't going to do that. I just wanted to teach you a lesson you'd never forget.'

'And you did, you did.'

Trip and Grace exchanged a long and incredulous look.

'That'll never happen,' Adam said. He removed the last wad of money then took a long breath and turned to Milton. 'But I'll never stop hoping you'll change your ways. Take this. It'll get you started again.'

Adam tossed the small wad of soggy bills to Milton's feet.

'Obliged.' Milton picked up the bills then shrugged. 'But doing what?'

'You seemed to enjoy running a saloon. You could do that again.'

Milton raised his chin, his eyes glazing as he pondered, then nodded.

'I *did* enjoy doing that, but Trip owns Calloway's Crossing now.'

Trip shook his head. 'I did.'

'Did?'

Trip considered the money in Milton's grasp then stood up to consider the duplicitous Milton.

'All the trouble I've faced has got me thinking that I ought to . . .' He looked at Grace, but her eyes were cold and she didn't even look at him. He shrugged. 'I ought to move on. Calloway's Crossing was your land.'

Milton's eyes lit up. 'That mean you'll give it back to me?'

'Not *give*.'

Milton nodded slowly then waved the wad of bills at him.

'I'll pay you two hundred dollars for your land and the saloon.'

'Make it a thousand and you got yourself a deal.'

Milton's mouth fell open with what Trip took to be genuine surprise.

'I ain't got that much money.'

Trip turned on his heel. 'In that case I'll talk to Marshal Kaplan before I leave and explain what you did. Even if Baxter did the most wrong, I reckon you've broken enough laws to get you a good long time in—'

'I understand,' Milton shouted. 'But Adam's only given me about two hundred. I just ain't got one thousand dollars, honestly.'

'You don't know the meaning of the word,' Trip said as Adam grunted his agreement. He turned to consider Milton and lowered his voice. 'But I tell you what I'll do. How much money have you got?'

'Including this, I got around three—'

'Be honest,' Trip snapped, pointing at Milton, 'or all deals are off.'

Milton and Trip locked gazes. Milton was the first to look away.

'I got about five hundred,' Milton murmured.

Trip reached into his pocket and withdrew the envelope Milton had given him three weeks ago. He held it out.

'Then that's my price for Calloway's Crossing.'

'But I need money for stock and for—'

'Then you'll just have to borrow the money.' Trip smiled. 'Let's hope the people around here will trust you enough to do that.'

Milton gulped. 'I got no hope.'

'Not my problem,' Trip said as Adam laughed at Milton's predicament.

Milton looked at the heap of money then at Adam, venturing a small smile, but Adam shook his head and dragged the money closer to him.

'All right, all right,' Milton said, his shoulders sagging. 'I guess you deserve to have your revenge on me, too.'

Trip held out a hand. 'Making someone honest ain't revenge.'

'But how will anyone ever trust me?' Milton asked, as he counted bills from various pockets into Trip's hand.

'For a start you could rename Calloway's Crossing and prove the double-crossing has ended.' Trip chuckled, remembering the sight of the saloon he was selling sinking into the mud. 'Or perhaps not.'

Milton placed the last bill into Trip's hand, and Trip slapped the envelope into Milton's hand.

'At least I got my land back,' Milton said, as he closed his grasp around the envelope. 'And I got me a profitable saloon.'

'Yeah. I got a good feeling about you.' Trip pocketed the money then shook Milton's hand. 'I reckon that saloon and you were meant for each other.'

Milton tipped his hat to Trip then to Adam and Grace, but nobody returned as much as a smile. Then he headed to his horse, his pace picking up, perhaps as the thought of returning to Calloway's Crossing took root, and by the time he was heading out of the gulch, he was whooping. Adam stood to watch him leave, the bag of money clutched to his chest.

'What you planning to do now?' Trip asked, as Adam headed to his horse.

'I'm getting as far away from Milton as I can before

he discovers what you've done to him.' Adam mounted his steed. 'And are you really moving on?'

Trip glanced at Grace. She still wasn't looking at him, but he raised his voice as he pointed down the trail.

'No. I'm heading to Wagon Creek.' Trip patted the bulge in his pocket. 'I reckon I've got enough money now to open a saloon there.'

Adam tipped his hat. 'Then I wish you luck.'

And with that, Adam galloped out of the gulch, whooping with even more excitement than his brother had. Trip watched him leave then paced round to stand before Grace. He ventured a smile.

'It'll be hard to run a saloon in Wagon Creek on my own.'

'It will.' She looked up at him, frowned, then stood and headed to her horse. 'But it won't be as hard as getting my help to run it.'

He watched her mount her horse and raise the reins, waiting for her to look at him again, but when she didn't, he hurried over to stand beside her.

'What do you want me to say?' he shouted up to her.

She looked down at him and for the first time in a while, she smiled.

'When you work that out, Trip Kincaid, you know where I'll be.'

She shook the reins and trotted out of the gulch. Trip watched her leave, her slow speed making him wonder whether she wanted him to catch up with her, but when he'd mounted his horse, he noticed that Frank Moore was loitering nearby. His hunched demeanour suggested he was looking for an opportunity to make amends for his actions, so Trip swung his horse past him.

'I'm mighty disappointed in you,' he said.

'I can't blame you.' Frank provided a rueful smile. 'And I guess I ought to apologize.'

'You ought to. And you can start by making sure that when your thirsty workers are looking for entertainment they head to Kincaid's Saloon.'

'I'll do just that. Calloway's Crossing will—'

'Not there. I'm opening a new saloon in Wagon Creek. And for your men, the first drink is free.' Trip narrowed his eyes. 'Provided they apologize.'

'For a free drink, that'll be no trouble.' Frank stood tall. 'And I'll be the first to say I'm sorry.'

Trip nodded then swung his horse round to leave the gulch. He rode quickly, hoping to catch up with Grace, but when he reached the trail to Wagon Creek he saw that several hundred yards on, she'd stopped and had turned her horse to look back towards him.

'Trouble is,' he said, as he slowed to give himself more time to think, 'I reckon my apology won't be as easy to make as that one was.'